AF663333

That Sounded Good When I First Thought of it...

A collection of short stories

notionpress
.com

That Sounded Good When I First Thought of it...

A collection of short stories

Abhimanyu Sheshashayee

notionpress.com

Notion Press

5 Muthu Kalathy Street, Triplicane,

Chennai - 600 005

First Published by Notion Press 2015

Copyright © Abhimanyu Sheshashayee 2015

All Rights Reserved.

ISBN: 978-93-84878-33-7

This book has been published in good faith that the work of the author is original. All efforts have been taken to make the material error-free. However, the author and the publisher disclaim the responsibility.

No part of this book may be used, reproduced in any manner whatsoever without written permission from the author, except in the case of brief quotations embodied in critical articles and reviews.

Hello Reader,

Like you, I too enjoy a good story. Any story. I don't really have a favourite genre; I just enjoy diving in and immersing myself in the story.

I find stories to be a complex and intriguing art form. To me, there are two parts to any good story. First, there need to be some interesting events to be relayed to the audience. At the very least, interesting events can make it easier to write a good story. I would find it difficult to write a story about watching paint dry. Second, the events in question need to be relayed in an engaging manner. Stories have numerous presentation elements and tropes that can really draw the audience in.

Since I was a child, I have taken a special interest in analysing storytelling. I enjoy crafting plots and exploring the nuances of narratives. The following is a series of experiments with storytelling. From school assignments to birthday presents, these are some of the stories that I have built over the years.

I want to thank my family, friends, and language teachers for their support and teaching.

I would also like to mention the website TVTropes.org for its fascinating compendium of information on the elements of storytelling. If you ever need a wiki on the art of storytelling, you should check out TVTropes.

Finally, there are innumerable authors that have contributed to my interest in stories. Above all, the author who inspired me the most was the legendary

Isaac Asimov. I don't consider myself a fan of anything – mainly because I never seem to know what being a fan entails – but if there was ever something I would be a fan of, it would be the works of Isaac Asimov. If you haven't already, go buy and read all his books. Every one of them. Start with the short stories. However, make sure you read his work after you read mine, or else you may feel thoroughly let down by my stories.

Contents

The Nightmare

This was a very early story of mine. I wrote it for a homework assignment in middle school, in my early teenage years. This was an exploration of three concepts that, being a child, I had just recently discovered. The first was how the method of narration can affect thc conclusion of the story. The second was the re-illustration of story from mythology; specifically Hindu mythology. The third was the idea of presenting the story from the perspective of an antagonist, and an understanding of why they would do what they do, but without either demonising or justifying it.

Humans. Many humans. An army of humans. Other creatures too. Many creatures. So many.

Approaching.

Approaching steadily. Approaching fast. Angry. Fury so great that it leaks out of their hearts and their mouths. A scream, a cry, a blast of trumpets. Vengeance. Revenge. They need revenge. They want what was taken from them.

Their leader is young, but he has a divine, ethereal aura surrounding him. He is filled with passion. He wants vengeance. He wants to take back what was his. Was it still his? He has doubt, but little doubt. He has faith. He has trust. He has courage. He has skill. He believes...

They build a bridge. No. This is not... this cannot be. They are coming fast. They are coming faster. Too fast. I must help. I need to help them. A clash of drums. The thunderous roar of a thousand drumsticks and feet beating onto leather skins and the ground, simultaneously. They have almost... they have arrived.

They commence their attack. They march forth. They begin to fight. To raid. To pillage and plunder and ravage and rape.

They are repelled. Pushed back. Desolated. We fight back. They will fall! They are flushed out! Destroyed! Gone... forever? No... They will return. Return again.

They return. Again. They fight. Again. Slaughter, be slaughtered. Once more are they fended off... but they return again? Again and again. We are growing weaker. Their numbers are great. Too great. Their presence is incredible. Their determination is intimidating. Their numbers seem infinite. Innumerable waves bearing down hard...

I must help!

This cannot be. They are getting closer. We get weaker. Weaker and more tired. Exhaustion. They... they are winning?? This cannot be! I must help! No! I need to help! Why can I not?! I am tormented! I watch in agony as my land is fertilised by the blood of its children. So much death...

Why? Why the carnage? Why the massacre? Why the hate, the malice, the war? Why?? This cannot be happening, yet I know it is. I must help, but I am unable to. I am shackled by my own foolishness; my own incoherence. I was betrayed! I cannot help my people because I was betrayed! WHY?! NO! They are too close!

The sounds of trumpets grow louder, as do the drums of war. The sounds of battle are upon me, yet I am unable to move! I am bound by a web of helplessness, the sticky material binding be to the bottom of the earth. The heat of a thousand suns and the frost of the breath of the gods washes over me, fatiguing my numbed senses. Fatiguing the web. I am slowly tearing out of it. I am breaking free! I will help… no… I have not yet finished recharging. I am not yet ready… but I must help! The web tried again to grasp me with its iron clutches, but I won't let it. The cold waters of the ocean currents pour over the web, loosening its strands. I am ripping, tearing, breaking… FREE!

I sit up, omniscient. To my left stand a number of worried servants, holding jugs of water, instruments and… my equipment. Armour and weapons. Refined and polished. Ready for battle. As I am.

I know what must be done. I get out of bed with speed I have never known myself. I grab my armour, donning it with haste. I take my weapons and sheathe them, ready to remove and wield them again. I rush out of the room, charging through the halls until I enter the throne room. My brother sits there, his face a mask of worry. I do not care; the fool has brought this upon himself, threatening us all. He looks at me and I look at him. His face is, for a single moment, covered with infinite relief, but then it hardens and becomes the cold, sovereign mask of integrity it always is. Almost always. He speaks:

"Kumbakarana..."

I interrupt him. "I am ready" I say. He nods. He knows as much as I do that I am not, as Brahma's boon bestowed, immortal, as I have not slept for the 6 months which I mistakenly agreed to, because of Vishnu's interference. I am ready, nonetheless, as I have stated. I turn and head for the stables. To my chariot. To the raging battle field. Lanka give me strength: today I will avenge you or die trying...

The Prize

> Also written in my early teens, this was an exploration of hopelessness and injustice. It uses a rather, well, melodramatic setting, but it tries to explore the depths of frustration begotten by perceived failure.

Murali stared at the letter, his brain going numb. His life's work, down the drain. How much he had put into this..... all the effort, all the time, all the work....... wasted. How? How could this happen? This could not be happening, it could not be possible. Every four years the world's scientific and medical community sent in their best ideas on medicine or biological sciences. Last time's winner had been Dr. Jacob Brown for the cure of Cyto-cystonic Cancer. This time Dr. Murali Sharma had entered with high hopes.

Dr. Murali Sharma had begun his research 30 years ago, 2 years before this Award had been instituted. Its official name was the World Medical Research Convergence Organisation, but it was to medicine as the Olympics was to sports. It was ultimately a competition. In fact, Murali had dedicated his life to entering this competition, not for the prize money of US$ 1 million, but because the winning entry would be converted into a fully funded international research project.

In truth, Murali hadn't even expected to get in the top 10, let alone win. However even if he got a place in the top 500, his research would be given some notice sooner or later; but he hadn't expected this. Not after all that work, all that research, all that experimenting. All of it for what? Nothing. His eyes fell on the letter again and he jerked them away; it hurt too much to read the letter. To see the letter. Even though the word was in a small font he could see it as if it covered the entire page. It was etched in his mind, his soul. It was the description of his life's work – Rejected.

He had not come 100th, he had not come 1000th. The world's scientific minds had deemed his work not even worthy of looking at. He sat in his bed for hours, unable to sleep, the letter lying on his lap.

"What do I do? What can I do?" he thought. At midnight, his hand involuntarily reached for his bottle sleeping pills that he kept on his bedside table.

Giovanni Bertrand, the Director of the World Health Organisation, sat in his limousine, staring at the sunrise through the tinted windows. He was going to a Dr. Murali Sharma's house to personally congratulate him on his winning the first prize in the World Medical Research Convergence Organisation. He had just been on the phone with Hans Grier of the Alfred Nobel Trust. Dr. Murali Sharma's work had been documented and had been approved for a Nobel Prize. What a man, what a mind! His Universal cure for AIDS had not only been a revolutionary idea, it had also been tried and tested by Swiss doctors and had been found to be successful. Two birds with one stone! The only worry was what

Dr. Sharma's reaction to this would be, as he was 50 years old and did not have a heart in perfect condition. Giovanni Bertrand had wanted to tell him personally of his achievement, but there had been a computer error and a letter had been sent to Dr. Murali Sharma. As the computer had deleted the soft copy of the letter, it was not certain what had been sent to Dr. Sharma, but Giovanni would tell him everything.

Dr. Murali Sharma, Nobel Laureate and winner of the First Prize in the World Medical Research Convergence Organisation, discoverer of the Universal cure for AIDS was found dead in his house, apparently suicide. He had taken an overdose of sleeping pills. Post-mortem analysis revealed over 660g of sleeping tablet matter in his stomach.

He was mourned as one of the greatest scientists the world had ever known.

The Final Journey

> I enjoy twists just as much as the next person. Ok, maybe more than the next person. Or the person after that. Or all the people after that. In any case, this is a fun story that I wrote for the express purpose of having a twist.

With a heavy heart I turned for a final glimpse of the ground I loved so much. The soil, the planet, the land that was mine. The dry sands were slaked with rivulets of limestone and from the distance of a moon from the planet, I stared out of the star-ship at the floating orb that was my home. I looked at the chronometer on the wall, just above the portal that I was standing at. Very little time left. Too little. Time always flies fastest when you don't want it to. I sighed deeply, thinking of all I would be leaving behind: my home, my people, my friends my family….. All for a greater cause.

It had begun many years ago, that is if you could define a year as the complete revolution of our planet around the sun. It was they who found us first. Officially at least. Their presence was officially declared after they sent probes right into our most populated cities. How they found us was yet to be discovered. We had always assumed that the probes we had, in our secret military installations out in the desert, were from other stars, maybe other galaxies. We never assumed they would come from our own solar system, from a planet adjacent to ours. Of course, there were conspiracy theorists who believed that Giant Green aliens from that planet would one day invade ours.

It all came down to one thing, however. They had sent us a message. It was a crude animation that had been carried by one of their probes. But it was a message no doubt. Now we were responding -- but not in like. Some nitwit had thought of sending a team of "trans-species ambassadors" to parley with those creatures. We would bc put into an artificially induced hibernation as thc ship's computer navigated its way to their planet. We, the crew, were not to wake up for another two years, and would never see our planet again. This was to be a one-way trip. Yes, we would be honoured as pioneers of Interplanctary Diplomacy, but at what cost?

A loud wail interrupted my stream of thought. I looked at the chronometer again. It was time. Time to leave for the alien planet. Time to leave for ever. Time to get into the hibernation units in which we would sleep until we reached the third planet from the sun. I stared momentarily at the red orb that was my planet, and her two moons. Then I retracted my optical sensors and slid into the hibernation chamber.

Machinations

> Following the theme of writing about Hindu mythology but with portraying elements in a different light, I wrote this story. It's a lot more technical than my other stories, and struggles to incorporate a twist. The goal here was to 'demythify' a particular aspect of Hindu mythology; that is, retell the story but without any magical/divine elements. I personally enjoy a good demythification. For me, a protagonist's divinity detracts from a story. I find that having a divine protagonist, one who was 'chosen' by the nebulous whims of a grandfathered-in deity, to be trite. I prefer to have a protagonist who steps up out of altruistic ambition, and whose divinity is replaced with intelligence, planning, and thinking out of the box.

"So are you going to tell me where we're going?" I asked.

"In a bit, in a bit…" replied my younger brother, in his classical enigmatic manner. "But first, I want to ask you a question"

I nodded. This was his standard way of answering a question: with another question that's coated with dramatic flair.

"So…" my brother started. "…what do you think is the reason for the superiority of humans, in the natural order?"

I stared at him blankly. Not because I did not have an answer, but because I was utterly perplexed as to where he might be going with this. I could not even begin to predict what was going on in his head. I had no choice but to play along.

"Well… our intelligence… for one thing. And… what about our ability to hold things in our hands?" I replied.

My brother snorted in mock derision. "Mice and monkeys can hold things in ways that people can't even imagine. And even dogs are smarter than humans: they hunt in packs, they eat what they can, and they don't pray…"

I nervously glanced around, reflexively. Talking ill of religion was never taken well. Not in this day and age. My worry was completely unnecessary, though: the insides of the luxurious caravan were as empty as the vast stretches of farmland that quickly slid by, around us; and the mahouts tending to the elephants pulling our caravan would be too busy watching the road ahead to even care about what either of us was saying. Furthermore, my younger brother was the uncontested lord and master of this region, and could get away with saying anything. I looked back at him, ignoring his fallow humour, and waited for his opinion on the matter. After all, that was why he had asked the question in the first place.

"Fire…" he said, his eyes solemnly closed. "…and scripture" he concluded, inhaling serenely after the last word: a dramatic pause. He could be a really good performer, when he wanted to be. It was why people were so ready to love him. He never gave a speech; he informed people of what they had always believed. Even I didn't have complete impunity to his charms, and I had grown up with him. I was intrigued by his pronouncement and wanted to hear what he was getting to. Nevertheless, I was not going to give in so easily.

"Fire, I can see" I said. "It's the manipulation of raw energy – something that no other creature does. But scripture? You mean like religious scripture? You think religion is the reason why humans are superior to animals? Didn't you just dismiss religion as something that even dogs were too intelligent to indulge in?"

"Yes… I mean, no…" My brother frowned, opening his eyes. I smiled inwardly: I had unbalanced him. "I mean, yes to the last question and no to the first two" he clarified. "I don't mean scripture to be religion, nor do I think religion is in any way responsible for human superiority" he said, ending his sentence with a touch of vivaciousness. "No, I mean that the ability of humans to create… doctrine. Humans can create their own laws and their own beliefs. That is a powerful tool…"

It was my turn to frown. "You're telling me that human laws are what make humans superior to animals?" I asked, with some vindictiveness. "The same laws which can and have deemed us as inferiors, because we came from a wandering tribe?"

"The very same" he replied, to my perturbation.

I shook my head in bewilderment. "How can you say something like that?" I asked. I was more confused than upset, as I knew my brother well enough to know that he wasn't into segregation of any sort, what with being from an 'inferior peoples' and all that.

"You misunderstand me" he replied, calmly. It wasn't a condescending calmness, as that would only serve to infuriate his audience, and he would never let that happen. It was a calmness mixed with a touch of pathos and a streak of determination, like he was the underdog who was trying to make a noble statement. "I mean laws as a tool. A tool of ordinance. You can use a plough to make furrows in earth or flesh, but that doesn't make the plough either correct or wrong"

"Fair enough" I agreed. "And that's also an interesting use of a plough"

"Humans have the ability to… to convince each other of rules. Rules that don't have to be followed. Rules that aren't needed to live…" He looked at me to see if I was following. I nodded. He continued: "In the natural order… with dogs and monkeys and mice… there are only the rules of survival. An animal does what makes it happy, whether that is eating, drinking, or siring young. A human does what other humans tell the human to do. And if the human is informed of something with enough authority, they will do it, even if it makes them unhappy" I nodded again, this time of my own accord. I could see his point, even if I had no idea where he was going with it. At the back of my mind, I wondered if I would eventually have to remind him of my original question, but right now I was interested in what he was getting at. "It is with these unnatural rules that humans can create the foundations of much more complex and powerful social structures than animals can" He looked at me with a glint in his eye. I could tell he had devised a pronouncement. "Dogs hunt in packs, but humans hunt in armies" he said. It wasn't quite correct, but I understood what he meant. Humans could organise and coordinate themselves much better than any animal. The converse was also true, but that was not important. I wanted him to proceed with his explanation.

"So what do fire and scripture have to do with where we are going?" I asked.

"I'll get to that in a bit" he said. "Do you know why I have chosen Bhismaka's daughter to be my bride?" he asked. "Besides her having the largest bosom you've ever seen" he added, with a sardonically mischievous grin. Bhismaka's daughter had such a flat chest that if she hid her face you could mistake her for a male.

"Because you secretly lust for men?" I retorted.

"If you think that a face like hers is in any way masculine, then you must be the one of us who wants men" he shot back. Before I could rebut him, he continued: "She is beautiful and all that, but no. It's because Bhismaka has cows"

I raised my eyebrows at that. "It's not good to speak of your future in laws in this way" I said wryly, and got a chuckle.

"No, I mean Bhismaka has the largest export of dairy products in the vicinity. It's his primary source of income, and his cattle farms are very well maintained"

I cocked my head, looking at my brother. If I didn't know that he could find a way to spectacularly implement any idea he had, I would have long dismissed his rants as that of a madman. Yet, time and again, he had put the most incredible plans into action and pulled them off with flying colours. What was he getting at here?

"So obviously, his second largest export is..." prompted my brother.

"Cow dung..." I said. Our childhood had been spent around our tribe's cows, so we both had quite some experience with them. Cows produced only slightly less dung than milk, which was logical, as they ate almost as much as they drank, if not more.

"Exactly!" he said with such exaltation that another listener would have been moved to tears of joy at being correct. "Now... what do you think the most important virtue is?" he asked. The sudden change in subject was unnerving, but I was used to it.

"Patience?" I asked dryly.

"Well, not quite, but I'll give it to you, since you said it earlier. Intelligence" he replied, ignoring my sarcasm. "But what about the second most important virtue?"

I stared at him blankly again. "The second most important virtue...?"

"What did Ma always tell us to do?" he prompted.

"What? Wash our hands? I don't know..." I said.

"To obey! Obedience is the second most important virtue" he said.

"Wait; how is obedience the second most important virtue?" I asked, perplexed.

"What, are you saying that Ma is wrong?" he asked irritated, but I knew he was not being serious. Before I could protest his obvious logical fallacy, he continued: "Now what if we apply these to laws. What do we get?" Again, he answered himself before I could: "We get understanding as the most important virtue – to understand the laws and their reasons – and we also get obeying the law as the second most important. Well, maybe not the second most important, but definitely up there" At this point, he started thinking aloud: "I guess contemplation would be important as well – to contemplate a law. And also industriousness, as procrastination is a bad thing. Hmm" He looked back at me. "Basically, a continuum between understanding laws and following laws – that could be construed as virtuous" he said to me.

"What are you trying to do? Start your own religion?" I asked.

"Not quite…" he said smiling, his eyes burning with inner fire. I knew that look. It was the look of his master stroke. I had inadvertently stumbled onto the crux of his plan. The crux of his plan was not quite starting his own religion? What did that mean?

"What do you mean?"

"When you can't sell your milk, find someone who is selling their milk and start selling your milk alongside them"

I was still confused, and my brother knew it.

"Basically…" he said. "I'm going to add my ideas to religion and sell it as religion"

I had so many questions at this point, but all I could say was: "And how are you going to do that…?"

"Well, you know, since religion is not like milk, you can't just pour one into the other" he said. "Religion is like metal, and to mix metals, you need…" he paused, as the caravan suddenly came to a halt. He was looking out of the window behind me, smiling, a look of pride on his face. I turned around, to look at what he was looking at, and my jaw dropped. Out of the window, I could that the caravan was perched at the edge of a cliff. A cliff that oversaw a massive factory complex, with numerous fiery smelters, burning furnaces, and strange domed buildings with spouts of flame gushing out of their tops, scattered across the expanse of the complex, all of which were, for some reason, releasing miniscule amounts of smoke. "…fire" I heard my brother say behind me.

After we disembarked from the caravan, my brother and I walked down to the factory complex. Troops stood at guard at various points. People scurried. There was an atmosphere of restrained haste. As we walked past, soldiers brought themselves to crisp attention and saluted. My brother acknowledged each salute with respect.

The building we approached was not a smelter or one of those strange domes, but was instead a massive thatched hut. The structure was palatial in size, but was constructed completely of loosely strung-together wooden rods and leaves. As we entered it, my brother explained to me that it was the testing chamber.

"Testing chamber for what?" I asked.

The inside of the structure was vast and hollow. Near our entrance were tables laden with bows and arrows, next to giant chariots that had a third wheel out in front, instead of a beam to which horses or elephants may be tethered. A giant stack of manuscripts stood behind the tables. The rest of the massive hall was empty and barren, except for the guards at the entrance. The light that filtered in through the interlaced leaves revealed massive burn scars on the grassy floor around the hall.

My brother went up to one of the tables and picked up a bow. He gingerly lifted an arrow from the table, paying attention to its tip, as he knocked it into the bow. He turned and indicated towards a target on the other side of the hall. Then, he aimed the bow, pulled back on the string, and let loose the arrow. Within moments, the arrow traversed the distance between my brother and his target. However, instead of the standard muffled 'thunk' that one usually hears, the target promptly transformed into a massive fireball. A tremendous shockwave of heat and light and sound burst forth, blinding and deafening me. Yet, a moment later, it was gone, and all that was left was... nothing. The target had disappeared altogether.

I turned to look at my brother in a mixture of horror and amazement, but he had put the bow down and was walking towards one of the chariots. I followed, watching as he quickly leapt onto the charioteer's dock, which was just behind the front wheel. Suddenly, a roaring filled the hall, as the chariot leapt forwards, as if it were being pulled by invisible elephants that were as fast as, no, faster than horses. The chariot raced forwards, to the far end of the room, before it swerved around and raced back, all in a matter of moments.

"How is this possible?!" I nearly yelled at him as he jumped off the chariot. He beckoned to me and pointed to one of the tables. This table had only one item on it: a strange wood and metal box, with multiple pipes and protrusions on it. He started walking towards the tablc and I followed behind.

"Remember what we were always told? Never approach the cows at night?" said my brother. "Because torches could suddenly explode when you went next to cows?"

"Yes!" I said. "Ba said it was because of the yakshas that…"

"It's because of cow dung" said my brother. "Let me show you"

When we reached the box on the table, he opened a small panel on the side. The strong, pungent smell of cow dung engulfed my sense of smell. At any other time, this would have brought back a flood of memories.

"The smell that comes out of cow dung – that smell is what can catch fire. But if you capture the smell, you can concentrate the smell and use the fire that it causes" he said. He closed the panel and headed towards the pile of manuscripts. We walked towards the pile, where he pulled a manuscript out and handed it to me. The top of the manuscript had the word 'Song of the Blessed Lord' neatly inscribed across it.

"With fire, scripture" he said. I looked up at him, curious. The pieces were coming together, but it was not quite complete.

"How does this fit in?" I asked him.

"Well, after we help the Albino King's sons defeat their cousins, we..." he started.

"Wait, what? Why them? I thought we were supporting the other side?" I said.

"Not when it comes to the crunch" he replied serenely.

"But why would we ever want to support those five brats?" I asked. "I mean, they're all horribly incompetent. One is a hedonistic pervert, one is a bully, and the eldest is quite content to gamble everything away... and the twins... they're complete pushovers! Their cousins are far more organised and far more competent, not to mention much smarter and more capable, and are so many more in number..."

"Exactly"

At that moment, it all fell into place. "The gods be damned..." I breathed. "So when the Albino King's sons... when they defeat the sons of the Blind King..."

"I didn't convince Devaki and Vasudeva that I was their long lost son, then kill Kamsa to become the ruler of Mathura, just so that I could be pushed around by the rulers of Hastinapura" he said. "Religion dictates that as the sons of a cowherd, we should be nothing more than mortal shells to be crushed by the wheel of time. But… we are more than that" He stepped back and flung his arms out. "Behold! The technology that will change fate itself!" He stepped forward again, clasping his hands as he did. "With this technology in the hands of our allies – and myself, of course, as the Pandavas are not smart enough to be entrusted these devices without supervision – I will take Hastinapura to be mine. Then, with the combined might of the plateau, we will be able to conquer all the kingdoms, from coast to coast! And finally, with fire, scripture: we will spread these scriptures across all the lands. We will deify ourselves! History will know us as gods amongst mortals!"

I shook my head, marvelling at the sheer audacity of the plan. "Krishna… you're crazy"

"No, Ramu…" Krishna replied, grinning maniacally. "I am divine…".

Distress

> This story is part of a much larger project that I have been working on for a while. The story itself is quite technical, as it is essentially an excerpt from a much larger setting. As such, this is really an exploration of world-building, rather than purely narrative.

Mining for fuel in space is always risky, especially when said fuel is an unstable radioactive compound. Now, contrary to popular belief, most very-heavy metals are not volatile – unless you decide to hit them with a neutron beam, in which case they undergo fission. The problem is that the mining operation uses high-power energy tools that sometimes result in sufficient excitation that the coefficients of critical mass are brought below the threshold of stellar radiation variance and... well, let's just say that accidental explosions occur quite frequently. For that reason, we have stringent safety protocols: if the outer layer of the energy armouring is breached, our vessel immediately performs a hyperspace jump, leaving behind all the mining drones. This is also why we stopped having piloted small-craft – it's much safer to use remote-controlled drones and just jump away when in trouble; but I digress.

I'm an engineer on the Hvrowrau. To be precise, I'm an Evaluator. It's second in command to the Architect. The Architect is the vessel commander. The Architect constructs a solution, the Evaluators evaluate components of the solution, and optimise wherever they can, and finally the Actors carry out the tasks, usually via the remote-control drones. For example, mining. We needed more fuel, so the Architect brought us to an asteroid belt around a class 6 star. Rich in very-heavy metals. Perfect fuel source. The Architect provided a schematic for our approach vectors. Since this is a civilian vessel – to be precise, a colony ship – I am the only Evaluator on board. Military vessels can have several Evaluators, but civilian ships don't need so many. So I evaluated the solution. Everything checked out; I optimised the operational parameters and relayed the orders to the Actors. The Actors piloted the drones through their intended trajectories, and the mining commenced seamlessly.

Sometimes, however, unforeseen problems arise. This time, it was a pulsar, several thousand light-cycles away. As we found out later on, it had long since died, but a beam of neutrinos, from one of its ancient pulses, arrived and bombarded the asteroid belt we were mining. We got sniped by a star's decaying corpse from across the galactic quadrant. Wonderful.

Well, the asteroid belt erupted, the Hvrowrau's energy armouring got instantly decimated, and we auto-jumped the hell out of there. All was well… or so we thought.

Most of our systems were down, due to the jump. Military vessels are outfitted with several backup reactor cores to prevent this: as soon as they jump in, they're ready for anything. However, a colony ship like ours tends to run out of energy after a jump. Only essential systems are left running, such as life support, energy armouring, navigation, and communications.

A quick check revealed that we were no longer in neutral space. We were sitting just over the border, in Cluster territory. Now, at the time, we didn't know very much about the Cluster, other than that they were a race of rogue machines intelligences that were at war with the Children. Since we, the Weave, were completely ambivalent to either the Children or the Cluster, this was not an issue for us. Yet, we always kept our distance. I'm not an expert at foreign policy, but it's usually never a good idea to enter another faction's territory, especially when that faction is a race of rogue machines that are at war with a faction of biologicals, especially since we're biological ourselves.

We had a bigger problem, however. When we had gotten hit by the explosions, our energy armouring had been breached unevenly: giant holes had been carved into the layers of armouring. Since this is energy armouring, it regenerates back to its original shape. However, a shard from the exploding asteroid belt had gotten wedged between our innermost layers of energy armouring, and was now stuck there. To make things worse, our sensors indicated that the shard was at a critical mass and excitation level. Finally, since most of our non-critical systems were down, there was really no way to extricate the shard. We had a bomb stuck to us.

So we sent out a distress signal.

First, we broadcasted it to only our Strand. Each strand is a different sub-faction within the Weave. Within our species, we have our differences of opinion. Rather than fight over them, we decided to split up into Strands. Together, the Strands comprise the Weave. Oh, and our Strand is the best Strand. Obviously.

After getting no replies from any of our Strand's vessels, we broadcasted the distress signal to the entire Weave. Still no replies. None of our vessels were in the vicinity –for the obvious reasons.

I discussed the problem with the Architect.

"We have to broadcast publicly." I said.

"No, that is not prudent." they said.

"We have no choice – we have civilians on board." I said.

"What if the signal is picked up by the Maw?" said the Architect. "They will slaughter us all, especially since we're a civilian vessel." We've been at war with the Maw for as long as I can remember. Not all-out war, as we're at opposite ends of the galaxy. However, they take every opportunity they can to commit atrocities against us. There have been several massacres of our civilians. To have a Maw vessel find us now would mean certain death.

"Possible, but improbable." I mused. "This is Cluster territory, and the Maw are biologicals. Logically they would stay away from border."

"Yes, but the Maw have a history of marauding, even over borders." countered the Architect.

"If I remember correctly, the Maw just recently signed a non-aggression pact with the Children." I pointed out. "If anything, that's bound to enrage the Cluster, which should keep the Maw away from here."

"And what if the signal is picked up by the Cluster?"

"We humbly beg them for assistance, and tell them that we're sworn enemies of the Maw, who are allied with the Children."

Ultimately, we decided to broadcast the distress call publicly.

It wasn't much later that a Telurbian vessel hailed us. The Telurbians are a minor faction: they primarily engage in trade and smuggling. After all, one faction's currency is another faction's contraband. In any case, they posed no threat. Their communication codes checked out, and a scan of their vessel matched its specs to those of a trade frigate.

"What seems to be the problem?" queried the frigate. The communicator sounded like a fellow Zyke; they even had the same accent as our Strand. It was not uncommon for other races to have Zyke crew members – you'll have a difficult time finding better navigators and engineers than us.

While the Weave is exclusively composed of Zyke, quite a few Zyke choose to work outside the Weave. They usually still pledge their allegiance to their Strand, and through their Strand, the Weave; but a source of credits is a source of credits. I have considered working freelance myself, but I my streak of nationalism tends to win. There's nothing quite like serving one's Strand.

We explained the issue to the Telurbian vessel. We thought that perhaps their vessel commander was listening in on the conversation but did not speak, for we only communicated with the Zyke voice on the other end.

"We can help." said the voice on the other end.

Maintaining the line, the Telurbian vessel moved in an arc, until the Hvrowrau's aft faced it. An energy spike registered, but from an unknown source. What were they doing?

A warning sounded. The energy armouring was ruptured. A narrow hole had been carved into the armour, right above the lodged shard. What had carved the hole? Correction: what was carving the hole? Something was burrowing into the energy armouring, creating a rift that was the exact shape of the shard. The rupture was nearing the innermost layer of armour. If that was breached, the Hvrowrau's hull would be exposed. However, with surgical precision, the rupture stopped at the exact point it reached the shard. The shard began to move out of the armour, sliding perfectly out of the breach. Soon, it was outside the armouring. The breach began to recede. Whatever had caused it was no longer doing so, and the energy armouring was regenerating.

"Is this sufficient?" asked the voice over the hail.

"Yes, thank you." replied the Architect. "But how exactly did you do that?"

“Gravitic ordinance.” replied the voice.

The Architect and I exchanged bewildered looks. Gravitic ordinance: generating concentrated gravitational fields to manipulate matter and energy. Could be used as a tool, or as a weapon. An age-old concept, but only the Cluster had figured out how to efficiently generate or control gravitational fields in such a manner. How had the Telurbians gotten hold of such technology?

Our confusion was cut short by a warning message on our scanners. A new vessel had arrived in our vicinity. A Maw ship. It was directly between the Telurbian vessel and the Hvrowrau. Scans showed it to be a Maw battle-cruiser. Marauders, no doubt.

“I need full power to jump drives.” ordered the Architect, building a solution on their console. I immediately relayed their orders to the Actors. “Telurbian vessel, you might want to consider jumping into neutral space.” said the Architect across the hail.

“Negative, Hvrowrau.” responded the voice. The Architect and I exchanged another bewildered look.

“Telurbian vessel... how do you know our designation?” asked the Architect.

In the meantime, the Maw battle-cruiser had closed in. It slowed and launched a missile. A single missile. The Maw specialised in missile ordinance. The loved launching missiles in flurries. The only reason why they would launch a single missile is if it were a siege-class missile. A scan revealed that the missile had no detectable warhead, which could only mean that this was an anti-matter tipped missile. That's the thing about anti-matter: it doesn't matter if it's anti-hydrogen or anti-uranium – the annihilation releases equal energy. So a missile with no discernable warhead – especially when launched in singular by a Maw battlecruiser – is bad news.

The missile covered the distance between the Maw vessel and the Telurbian vessel within nano-clacks. They both disappeared from our scanners. Then the weirdest thing happened: on our scanners, in place of the Telurbian vessel appeared a Cluster vessel. The designation was unknown, and our scanners could not make head or tails of its specs. Later on, one of our Actors told me that they had gotten a visual of the detonation. They told me that they had seen the tail of the missile, like a comet, and then an incredible flash of white light. In front of the light stood a silhouette of an enormous vessel, the size of a dreadnought class, with giant tendrils extending from it. They told me that they saw its energy armouring rippling in the blast, with no apparent breaches, even in its outermost layers.

That's when we noticed, on our scanners, that the shard of fuel was moving. It arced away from the Hvrowrau, and sped around the Cluster vessel, coming around and into the Maw battleship. Gravitic ordinance. Predictably, both the shard and the Maw vessel disappeared from our scanners. Unlike the Telurbian vessel, the Maw vessel did not change into something else. It simply vanished.

The events that followed were complex, but I'll give you the short version.

The Cluster vessel stayed in the vicinity until the Hvrowrau was back to full capacity. We jumped out of Cluster space, and headed back to our primary dock. We were later sent on another colony mission, but this time to a system on the other side of Weave territory, which had only a single gas giant. We're currently in the process of colonising the gas giant.

Following the incident, the Weave and the Cluster set up a diplomatic exchange program, which was met with a degree of success. Due to our conflict with the Maw, and the war between the Cluster and the Children, and the non-aggression pact which had grown into an aggressive alliance between the Maw and the Children, the Cluster sought to ally with the Weave. The galaxy was divided into two sides, and is now poised on the brink of all-out war. Smaller factions all around are scrambling to seek refuge or capitalise on this looming conflict, which threatens to be like none other, while the main factions are gearing up for conquest.

So it begins.

The General and the Mathematician

The story pun or 'Feghoot' is a short story that builds up around and concludes with a pun on an adage. I find these kinds of stories to be quite hilarious. This is my attempt at a Feghoot.

When the nation of Supi waged war against its enemies, its armies were led by none other than General Jirvatax Itee. The general was a cunning man, and used complex manoeuvres and strategic positioning to route the foes of Supi. The general made sure that each task force under his command had a very specific role to play. For example, he would position the tank battalions in the forward, while flanking with cavalry, finally reinforcing with infantry. All in all, his tactical sense allowed Supi to gain many victories, and its armies marched forth, undefeated.

However, all this changed at the Battle of Kvaask, where the general's forces were routed, despite his keen strategizing. Stranded in the Kvaask fortress in the middle of the Akvurnian Jungle, the general could do nothing but wait and hope for reinforcements to arrive, while enemy forces besieged his position.

Back in Supi, the ruling council was in despair. Without the general to lead their forces, Supi would surely fall, and they did not know what to do. Even if they did replicate the general's methods of command, the enemy had found some way of countering those methods.

As the council debated their next action, an aide stood up. 'I know what to do', said the young lady. Having found no suitable alternatives, the council agreed to listen to the aide. The aide went to the front of the chamber, and began to explain.

The aide was a mathematician. Her idea was to take the strategies of the general, and change them. Where the general had used infantry in a specific position, the strategy should be changed to encompass the use of cavalry and tanks in that position, and so forth. Then the positions in the general's strategies could be randomly populated with the appropriate troops, and used in battle.

The council was sceptical, but agreed to try out the proposal. Before these tactics could be implemented in full scale, the mathematician would first have to locate and retrieve the general, from the Kvaask fortress. The mathematician agreed, and she set out for the Akvurnian Jungle with a moderate task force, which she could use to demonstrate her idea.

Upon reaching the Akvurnian Jungle, the mathematician drew up the plans for the modified strategies, and then relayed them to her task force. The infantry, cavalry, and tanks were given their randomly generated battalions, and each battalion moved to its appropriate position on the battlefield. Then, she gave the attack order, and the troops moved forwards.

The enemy, still laying siege upon the Kvaask fortress, was taken by surprise. Furthermore, their previous counters to the general's strategies did not work against the mathematician's battalions. The enemy was thoroughly defeated, and the Kvaask fortress was freed. The mathematician's troops moved in and secured the general and the other occupants of the fortress.

When the mathematician and her troops successfully returned to Supi, there was much rejoicing to be had. The mathematician was lauded as a hero, and she was given many accolades for her success. In her debriefing, only a single question was asked of her by the council: 'How? How did you manage to succeed?'. Her reply was succinct: 'Without loss of General Itee'.

How it happened

'How it Happened' (with a capital H for 'Happened') is a short story by Isaac Asimov. It's one page long and is one of my favourite stories ever. I'm not going to tell you what it's about; it's available online for free; go read it now. Just do a search for the title. You will love it.

In any case, my story is not the same. I did, however, ~~blatantly plagiarise~~ humbly borrow the title. To be fair to me that was because I wrote this story for an exam. Yes, this was written in half an hour. I was actually trying to write something completely different, but then tore up the latter pages of that arc and wrote this one.

Well, I hope you like it.

Bob sauntered through the woods, stumbling a bit. He was tired. Sleepy. Haggard and worn. He'd been walking for quite a few days now, trying to navigate through the forest without getting lost or mugged. This forest was known for its bandits. Bloodthirsty bandits who, as the stories spoke of, were roving savages who mercilessly slaughtered travelling lords and stole their possessions.

The bandit problem was a rather sad one. Recent fluctuations in the economy had caused it. War, recession and general civil unrest had been the major causes. Moreover, the nation's supreme leader had, like any aristocrat, indulged himself while leaving everyone else to rot. Due to this, so many poor souls had turned to crime to avoid starvation. Bob could actually feel pity for them, as he was on the verge of doing the very same. Unemployed, his house foreclosed on, no family to turn to, sufficient training in weapons and tactics when he had been an officer of the law, Bob was a prime candidate for turning to crime. He thought about it more often than he felt comfortable with.

Nevertheless, whether or not to become a bandit was, right now, not as important as whether or not to become a bandit's victim. He had to stay alert. The night was the only time he could travel safely – since contrary to popular belief, bandits preferred to ambush travellers in the day and sleep at night – but even then, he didn't want to bump into any bandit dens or something like that. No, he had enough problems already without actually walking into a bunch of sleeping bandits.

So Bob plodded onwards. Slowly, painstakingly, straining his eyes in the darkness before putting a foot forwards carefully. He couldn't afford to use a torch, as that would be just calling for a mugging. He couldn't afford to make too much noise, lest he were heard by some nearby wandering bandits. He had to move silently and stealthily.

Easier said than done.

Winter was setting in fast. Too fast. While the first snows were yet to fall, the cold northern winds were ravaging the land. The night was the worst, with the cold at its bitter peak. The darkness exacerbated the cold, making the journey incredibly difficult to bear. The biting chill dug its fangs into Bob's legs, as he trudged through the murky black of the forest.

It was around midnight when Bob saw the bonfire. After several hour of the monotonous and frigid travel through the woods, Bob was exhausted beyond measure. He was all but frozen solid and was ready to drop where he stood. Bandits or no bandits, he had to get to that fire. If not, there was a good chance that he'd never make it out of the forest alive. So, with renewed vigour, Bob set out for the fire.

After a few gruelling minutes of trudging through the cold shrubbery, Bob finally reached the fire. He could feel its warmth envelop him as he approached it. He could feel his body start to thaw as he came close to the fire, stretching his hands out to bask in its warmth. He could feel the yellow glow pierce into his eyes, blinding him temporarily, as his eyes adjusted to the brightness.

Unfortunately, his elation was short lived. When he opened his eyes after a few moments of enjoyment, he found that he had – obviously – walked right into a bandit camp. Well, he had kind of expected it to happen sooner or later. The only question was what was going to happen now.

There were three bandits sitting around the fire, staring at Bob. He could tell that they were bandits because of the numerous weapons that they had by their side, as well as because of the eye-patch on the fat, robed man who happened to be closest to Bob. The other two bandits were dressed in camouflage green, one being a thin and short fellow while the other being humungous and heavy-set. Even against just these three, Bob doubted his chances, yet he knew that they would not be sitting here alone. It only looked that way. From some experience, Bob knew that the rest of the bandits were probably nearby, sleeping some distance from the fire, while a skeleton shift worked to keep the fire alive at night. It was the standard operating procedure for most military outfits, and so would have been the logical choice of procedure for the bandits as well. In any case, fighting was out of the option. Diplomacy was the only way to go.

"Hi there" said Bob, hoping to mask his nervousness with a casual tone.

The three bandits looked at each other, then looked back at Bob. Their expressions were unreadable.

"What are you doing here?" asked the fat one suddenly. Bob looked at him. This man had once been clergy of some kind, Bob could tell. The one-eyed bandit had a plump stature and wore priestly garbs which looked as moth-eaten and worn as his eye-patch.

"Looking for some company on this cold night" said Bob cheerily. Maybe, just maybe, if he acted like an idiot, the bandits would let him go thinking him a drunkard or a fool. Then again, they might just use him as target practice. One could never tell with bandits. Even so, Bob decided that being cheery was probably his best bet.

"I know you..." said the fat bandit suddenly.

Bob looked around him, wondering who he was talking to. The bandit couldn't surely know Bob. Almost no one knew Bob. Even so, the fat bandit seemed to be addressing Bob himself. Bob was perplexed, and somewhat curious.

The fat bandit continued: "I knew your father. Knew him very well" he said, in a tone that did not connote any of the warmth that the words alone might have. In fact, the fat bandit seemed to be furious.

Bob was now utterly dumbfounded. A trickle of fear ran down his back. Not only was he standing here talking to armed bandits, but he seemed to have annoyed one of them without even doing anything. Bob hadn't known his father himself, let alone know his father's old acquaintances. How did this bandit know Bob's father? How did he know that Bob was his son?

"He took my eye!" said the bandit hoarsely, pointing at his eye-patch. "Said he was just borrowing it from me. But he took it and never gave it back!" The bandit turned to fully face Bob. "I want my eye back!" he rasped.

Bob was now utterly terrified, but he struggled to not show it. This man was spewing insanity. Was he a drunkard or a fool himself? What was he talking about? Wanting his eye back? This was insane. This had to be some sort of joke... wait... what if it was? Bob suddenly realised that it was highly likely that this man was playing with him. Just as a cat plays with a mouse before killing it, perhaps. Perhaps not. Either way, Bob decided that two could play that game.

“Definitely, sir” replied Bob. “Pardon my father’s forgetfulness. He collected many eyes from many people, and probably forgot about yours. His collection is quite large, you see, and so I do not know how I will be able to find your eye in it. However, if you were to give me your other eye for comparison, then I would be able to search his store and find your eye for you”

There was a brief moment of silence. Only the crackling of the fire could be heard, as all three of the bandits looked at Bob, their expressions still utterly unreadable. Bob struggled to not turn and run from there. He casually reached up and mopped his brow, pretending that it had developed from the warmth of the fire.

“Would it be an eye-terative process?” asked the large bandit suddenly. Bob and the other two bandits turned to look at the large one. The man was smiling broadly at his horrible pun.

Without warning, the small one and the fat one both burst into merry laughter, making a louder ruckus than Bob would have liked. Even so, Bob did not say anything because he still wasn’t sure if he was safe or not.

The large bandit suddenly got up and walked up to Bob. It took every gram of Bob’s willpower to not cower as the giant approached. However, instead of killing, maiming or decapitating Bob, the giant just extended his hand, still chortling.

“Well met, my man!” said the giant jovially. “Tuck has been playing his little trick on everyone. You’re the first to have beaten him at his own game”

Bob glanced back at the fat bandit, referred to as 'Tuck'. The man had taken off his eye-patch to reveal a perfectly healthy eye in its place. He too was smiling, albeit a bit sardonically. Bob mildly saluted him, before accepting the giant's handshake.

Moments later, Bob was sitting next to the fire, talking with the fat 'friar' Tuck, the massive 'little' John and the skinny man known only as Much. After Bob had explained his reasons for passing through the forest – to get to Nottingham, but via none of the common trade routes, which were all being watched by the Sheriff – John asked Bob where he was from.

"Well, I'm from the neighbourhood I was last in" replied Bob. He didn't want to disclose details about his origins, and he hoped the men would be able to respect that. "I'm just a man in the 'hood" he said.

"And what name do you go by?" asked Friar Tuck.

"Well, my real name is Robert, but I go by the names Bob. Or sometimes even Robin" replied Bob.

"Well, then..." said Little John. "Robin Hood. Welcome to the gang..."

Recursive

> This story was inspired by a part of the game Neverwinter Nights: Shadows of Undrentide. I wrote this story as a weird experiment with the concept of 'recursive reality'. It takes the idea of a story within a story, and makes it a lot more, well, freaky. I had fun with it; I hope you do too.

The two men walked into the laboratory.

"I call it the Dream Beam" the short man declared with triumphant flair, as the two of them entered the large, circular room. He gestured to the giant metallic pillar in the centre, emitting pulsing flashes and a soft crystalline hum. A dozen terminals encircled the towering device, with graphs and readouts. A number of technicians manned the terminals, with one moving back and forth between three terminals and a giant mainframe in the corner. The tone was generally hushed; none of the occupants of the room were even stirred by the grand entrance of the two.

The short man continued, with some hastened apology to his tone "Although it isn't really a beam. And it doesn't really have anything to do with dreams." He shrugged. "It just sounds better like that. More…" he gesticulated at the device with both hands. "More poetic."

The short man's companion looked at him, waiting for him to continue, as if to say 'so what does it really do?'. Seeing this look, the short man smiled, as a magician would smile before going from showing the audience a lady in a box to explaining that he would now saw the box in two.

"What it really does..." continued the short man, turning to look at his creation. "...is construct a sub-structural entanglement that can manifest a representation of a set of parameters that delineate the foundations of a conceptual metaphysics." The short man turned to look at the taller man. The latter's eyes had glazed over. The short man resisted the urge to roll his own, and instead tried to simplify his explanation. "It allows you to create an alternate reality... based on your thoughts" he said. His companion did not react at first. Then the taller man frowned.

"Create an alternate reality?" asked the taller man.

"Yes, generate an entire universe. Create a... a new plane of existence. From scratch" said the short man, excitedly. He turned back to gaze lovingly at his invention. Then he looked at his companion again. "As you can imagine, the possibilities are endless. In fact, the possibilities are limited solely by your imagination" he stressed on the last few words, grinning widely.

"I... well, this is impressive" said the taller man, his brow still furrowed. "But this is not what we gave you funds for" he continued. "We expected weapons..."

"You paid me for a knife" interrupted the scientist, indignant. "I made you a nuke. This machine can rewrite reality, for god's sake." The scientist closed his eyes and shook his head. He was astounded at how obtuse the taller man's statement has been. "This device can. Re. Write. Reality." The scientist was careful to enunciate each word. "How can you not see the potential in that?"

That caused a change in the taller man's expression. The politician narrowed his eyes and furrowed his brow even more. "Wait..." he started, slowly. "So, you're saying that..." The scientist nodded at him, prompting him to continue. "Using this device..." The politician paused again, and the scientist jumped in.

"If you wanted, you could turn all your enemies into incontinent sheep" suggested the scientist, his tone a cordial mix of humour and impatience. He wondered why the politician was taking so long to digest the ramification of this technology. The incredible, incalculable, wonderful and terrible ramifications of this nigh omnipotent technology.

The politician was silent for a moment. Then he started, slowly: "So..." He suddenly became more decisive: "Can you do that?"

"Do what... exactly?" asked the scientist, suddenly apprehensive. The politician did not reply, so the scientist ventured a guess. "Turn someone into a sheep?" The politician turned his gaze away from the towering device towards the scientist, then back to the device. "No!" barked the scientist.

The politician turned towards the scientist. His brow, which had been slowly smoothing erupted with a fresh set of creases. "You said that...!" he began, his tone a mixture of pathos and menace that could only come from a politician.

"I said that I would give you a demonstration!" the scientist retorted, before the politician could get a biting accusation in. The scientist continued: "I will show you how this device works, not demonstrate it usability as a weapon". The politician looked like he was about to protest. "Besides, it's still too dangerous to actually use as a weapon" said the scientist quickly. "It needs a lot more testing before we can use it to alter this universe. Right now it's set to not be able to directly affect this universe… this reality… just in case something goes horribly wrong." This explanation did seem to placate the politician. Both men turned to look at the humming device, simmering in their own thoughts for a brief while.

"So what can you show me?" said the politician at last, his tone neutral with just the slightest touch of disappointment and disinterest. He was instinctively trying to mask his interest, hoping to get the scientist to try harder to sell the device to him. He wasn't interested in having jargon thrown at him; he wanted something concrete. Something to work with. Even if it were – as the scientist has mentioned – turning people into sheep. That application alone, ludicrous as it sounded, could be used in a variety of ways. To rid the politician of many, many enemies. It wasn't that the politician was unimaginative; it was just that he was more used to using his imagination to fuel his political career, not to build fantastical gizmos in an ivory tower. No, for that, he had hired the scientist, and the scientist seemed to have delivered. Now he just wanted to milk the scientist for as much possible, specifically for concrete, easy-to-use power. He didn't care about the design and specification of the weapon; he just wanted to be able to point and shoot.

The scientist was only too glad to demonstrate the operation of his creation to the politician. He eagerly led the politician to an unmanned terminal next to the mainframe. There, he minimised the various performance and data-collection programs that were running in the background, and opened the core interface program. He grabbed a nearby empty chair and beckoned to the politician to sit down. Then, the scientist pushed himself away from the terminal, prompting the politician to go closer to it.

"What do I do now?" asked the politician, sitting at the terminal, facing a screen covered in numerous complex graphs and data readouts, much more so than the terminal had had previously. He didn't understand any of it, and not so unconsciously hoped that he would never have to.

"You formulate a reality" said the scientist. He reckoned that the politician would not understand him fully, so he continued before the politician could ask. "The device reads your thoughts and manifests – creates – a reality. A new reality. A… temporary alternate universe, if you will. You can do this in several ways, but one of the easiest is by defining some sort of fictitious narrative… say by reading a story aloud. Then, we can observe the creation of the new universe from here." The scientist gestured to all of the other terminals in the room. "The universe will be spontaneously generated by the device. Everything in it will be defined by your imagining of how the universe must be"

"Wait, so do I... have to imagine everything in the universe?" asked the politician.

"Ah!" said the scientist, smiling. "Great question. The answer is – thankfully – no. You don't need to imagine everything." The scientist spun himself around in his chair, looking contemplative. "This is one of the amazing things about this device – something that we're still investigating. The relationships between the existential and the existent. The current hypothesis is sort of..." The scientist paused, then looked at the politician. "Have you heard of Schrodinger's Cat?" asked the scientist.

"Only that it's a dead cat in a box" replied the politician "Except that it's not... really dead... or something like that..."

"Well, Schrodinger's Cat was a thought experiment about quantum uncertainty" said the scientist. "I won't go into the details, but the general idea was that, until the cat could be observed, it did not have a defined quantum state... that is, it could not be said if the cat was alive or dead... until it was observed"

"You mean like, if a tree falls in the forest...?" started the politician.

"Exactly!" cut in the scientist. "If you do not observe the tree, whether it has fallen or not is irrelevant, for the purposes of your understanding of the universe." The scientist spun towards the terminal and gestured. "This device builds a universe... or alters some universe... around your imagined properties of that universe. But it does so in a way that the rest of the universe does not affect... does not matter to the properties of the universe that you have imagined." The scientist glanced at the politician and saw that the latter had not fully grasped the meaning of the statement. "Consider..." continued the scientist, facing and gesticulating towards the terminal. "...if I imagined a universe that consisted of a lone rock on a grassy field." The scientist glanced back at the politician, who nodded at the scientist. The scientist turned back towards the terminal. "Now, this device would construct a universe that had... any properties. Any. Maybe there are stars and planets, like in our universe. Maybe there is a single flat world which rests on the back of a giant turtle. The point is... it doesn't matter. What would matter is that, somewhere in that universe, there would be a giant grassy field, and in the middle of the field would be a rock." The scientist looked at the politician again, who nodded again. "However..." the scientist said, still looking at the politician. "...what is important is that the rest of the universe will be created such that that grassy field and that rock would not be affected by anything else that exists in that universe." The politician nodded, understanding what the scientist was talking about. The universe that the device would create would be tailored to fit the specifications of the creator.

The politician considered this information for a moment. Then: "What about paradoxes?" he asked.

"Great question!" said the scientist, looking jubilant. "The answer is simply that we don't know. We don't know what would happen if you, for some reason, imagined a universe where a property was both entirely true and entirely false. Or if there existed a man who could only tell lies, who called himself a liar. Or a universe where someone went back in time and killed their parents before they were born. How those universes could even exist... well, that's why we're not going to risk... well... messing with this universe." The scientist gestured around.

The politician nodded, understanding. He looked back at the terminal in front of him. The array of ridiculously complex... stuff... still lingered on the screen, intimidating the politician. "Ok, so... do you have any suggestions as to what I do now?" he asked.

"Here, let me..." the scientist said, petering off. He pulled up to the terminal, causing the politician to scoot aside a bit. Quickly, he pulled up a text file, which he maximised on screen, covering all the graphs and data readouts, much to the politician's relief. Then, he slid back, allowing the politician to return to his position in front of the terminal. "It's an excerpt from a story" said the scientist. "Read it out loud, and then, when it ends, let your imagination carry you on"

The politician nodded. He squinted a bit, adjusting his eyes to the text. Reading unfamiliar documents out loud was something he had much experience with, as his staff, especially his speechwriters, could easily attest to. He cleared his throat and began:

"The two men walked into the arcane chamber…"

The new king and his vizier approached the glowing humanoid form that hovered in the middle of the large, circular room. The Unknowable One. The most powerful of magi in all the realms; a lich with no peer in control over the ethereal and arcane arts. From whence the renowned and feared being had come, no one knew. Nor was known its agenda, if any. All was known of it was that it existed in no world, yet in all, being one with the void between voids.

"So this is the one who will make all my dreams come true…" said the new king. He said it to no one, yet it was addressed to his vizier.

"Of course, sire" grovelled the vizier. "The Unknowable One is the most powerful being in all the lands…" The young king threw the vizier a scornful look. "…except for you, of course, my liege" the vizier corrected himself. "Your grandeur is without bounds"

The young king smirked, straightening his robes. He looked up at the floating figure. "Hey, you over there!" he called to it. "I demand you come before your king and pay me your respects!"

"My liege!" whispered the vizier, worriedly. "I would request… humbly, of course… that you do not speak to the Unknowable One so!"

"Shut up, underling" spat the young king, looking down at the vizier, utter disdain on his face. "I did not have my father disposed of so that I could be told what to do"

"Of course, my lord" said the vizier, meekly. "And it was I who assisted you with your task. Even now I continue to assist you, grandsire, but... but I think it would be in your best interests to let the Unknowable One speak..."

"Silence!" crowed the king. "I will do as I see fit!" He turned back to the floating figure in the middle of the room. "Is it not you who fulfils the dreams of the new king of the realm?" the king said to the floating figure.

Suddenly, a tremendously deep voice resonated across the room. "YES" rang the voice, appearing to emanate from the walls. The sound was so alien that it caused the king to fall silent, paling. "IT IS I WHO WILL GIVE YOU THE BOON OF POWER, LITTLE MONARCH" spoke the voice. If the king was aggrieved for being called little, he did not show it. "THE SPELL IS PREPARED" the voice continued. "WITH IT, YOUR EVERY THOUGHT WILL BE MADE MANIFEST UNTO REALITY" the voice finished.

There was a brief moment of silence. The king waited, not sure if he should speak. After a moment of gathering his wits, he broke the silence: "Ok... so how do I use this spell?" he asked.

"FIRST, THE SPELL MUST BE PRIMED" boomed the voice in reply, startling the king once again. "YOU WILL BEGIN BY RECITING FROM THE PARABLE OF THE MATRIARCH." A glowing scroll appeared in front of the king. He reached out and grabbed it. The voice continued: "THENCEFORTH, YOUR INNER

THOUGHTS MAY BE MADE CLEAR, AND THEY WILL SHAPE ALL OF CREATION AS YOU SO DESIRE" The voice paused once again. The king looked around, wondering what he was supposed to do. He glanced at the vizier, who looked as terrified as he felt. The vizier indicated to the scroll. The king looked at it. Perhaps if he began reading it… "BE WARNED" the voice suddenly boomed, causing the king to almost drop the scroll. "THE SPELL WILL RENDER THE EXACT NATURE OF YOUR DREAMS, WHETHER THEY ARE DISCIPLINED OR NOT." The voice stopped again. The king wondered if he should ask what that warning had meant, but his greed for power overcame him. He unfurled the scroll, and began reading aloud:

"The Matriarch walked into the cave of the altar…"

She held the seven blades of her spear aloft as she entered, in respect of the sanctity of the altar. She slowed her pace as she approached the crystal pillar, lowering her thorax and holding her sex open, in reverence. Her tendrils brushed against the ground, and she narrowed twelve of her twenty three eyes, as the elder teachings had instructed her. The altar beckoned. It was the One True Source, said to contain the very apex of the crystal-verse. It was the cornerstone of her life's ambition. The shimmering walls gleamed with the souls of trillions she had slain, in the name of purity. The cryolisks, the baryocytes, the ardyotes; even the larvae. She had slaughtered them all… all in the name of the altar. In the name of the One True Source. She had begun her holy quest over a thousand cycles ago, when she had fed on the still-living bodies of her parents and other kin, punishing them for their impure form. She alone had been born tri-circular: the holiest of holies; and her circularity – her purity – was found in none else. Thus, she had laboured, for hundreds of cycles, purifying all in her path, collecting their screaming souls in her maw, before retching them into the altar, and then copulating with it. It was hers... hers to maintain, to feed, to activate. Now, having purged the crystal-verse of the impure, she sought to perform the final ritual. The final intercourse. The final submission. All of the crystal-verse; indeed, all of creation would be hers. Hers to purify. Hers to make pure with but will. Her dream was about to reach fruition.

She laid her sultry form around the altar, preparing herself for the final conjugation. She admired her circularity, and pruned the perfection of her tri-cyclic form. She fondled the altar, slowly rubbing her unhinged maw against the infinitely hard crystal. The souls of the final departed, the last of the impure, the last of the living, flowed out in soft retches. She coated the pillar evenly with the final souls, embracing her circularity and the circularity of the altar; embracing it till they were one. She was one with the One True Source.

A vision began creeping into her mind. The altar was responding to her sacrifice. It was providing her a sensual, exotic dream, which bathed over her mind like she had bathed in the blood of the billions she had mercilessly executed. Slowly, the vision coagulated, from intangible mass into a specific visual form. Script. Text. The vision was text, bidding her to read it. If she started reading it, it promised her, she would soon be able to achieve completion. She would be made whole, made into a goddess... a divine entity of infinite power. As long as she retained her focus, her dreams would sculpt reality. She composed her mind into a form of appreciation. Then, she moved the text into focus, and began to read:

"The politician suddenly became aware of his surroundings..."

The text had come to an end. He looked up, and around. The room was now empty, but for himself and the scientist. The latter was sitting some distance away, worriedly glancing between terminals, looking at the various indicators on the screens. He suddenly noticed that the politician was no longer reading. He turned to the politician, a fearful look crossing his face.

"Listen to me very carefully" started the scientist, speaking quickly. "Whatever you do now, keep your mind clear. Don't think about anything"

The politician was puzzled. He wondered why. "What's going on? What's the problem?" he asked.

"There is no problem!" said the scientist, sounding not the least bit sincere. "Stop thinking!"

"Wait, but why?" asked the politician, concerned. He did not understand what the scientist was going on about. Then, a sudden thought entered his mind. "Wait, what did... how...?" he started, slightly unsure about how to put his question into words. Before the scientist could stop him, he continued: "How did we end up here?"

"I don't know what you mean" said the scientist, still sounding fearful and completely insincere. He knew exactly what the politician meant.

"You know exactly what I mean" said the politician. "How did we get here? I was reading a story – something about a king and a wizard or something. Then that king story read a story, about some crazy alien, and then that alien read a story... about... us...?"

The scientist grew still, staring in horror at the politician, his skin going pale. He gulped nervously. The politician noticed this, but had no idea what to make of it. Instead, he decided to continue on his line of questioning.

"So did we just read a story about ourselves... and make our own universe...? Did we even make a universe, or are we just... what did you call it? Rewriting our own reality?" The politician paused, considering the implications of what he had just asked. "Or are we even real? Did we just imagine ourselves imagining ourselves...? How does that even work...? It doesn't make sense..."

A cold horror swept over the politician as he realised the paradoxical nature of his contemplation. The scientist screamed in terror as the universe collapsed around the room, and the entire laboratory winked out of existence.

The Matriarch suddenly became aware of her surroundings. The text had come to an end. She looked up, and around the cave, wondering what she had just seen. The vision had been disturbing, to say the least. What did it mean? Was it a test? Was the altar testing her resolve? Had she not satiated it enough? She had purged the entire crystal-verse of life, since all of it was impure but for her… but it demanded more? She concentrated on the vision she had just had. She had created a world, an entire universe, with just her thoughts. That was the power that the altar had given her. Yet, it had also implied that she was, herself, just the figment of some other entity's imagination. How could that be? What was this more powerful entity? Then again, it had itself been imagined by an entity that she had imagined. Was there even such an entity? Was she even real? Did she just imagine herself imagining herself? How did that even work? It didn't make any sense…

A cold horror swept over the Matriarch as she realised the paradoxical nature of her contemplation. She tried to wail, but the sound was drowned out by the shattering of the crystal around her, and the cave of the altar crunched out of existence.

The king suddenly became aware of his surroundings. The text had come to an end. He looked up, and around. The Unknowable One was nowhere to be seen, and the chamber was empty, but for the vizier.

"What did I just see?" asked the king, to no one in particular, yet it was addressed to the vizier.

"I don't know, my… my liege…" stammered the vizier.

"Did I just read a story about… about me?" asked the king. "Did I just make… well, make reality?" he continued, confounded. "Am I even real? Is anything real, or is it all just a figment of someone's imagination? Could I be just a figment of my own imagination?"

A cold horror swept over the king as he realised the paradoxical nature of his contemplation. He could not tell if he or the vizier were screaming more, as the walls around them crumbled, and the chamber faded out of existence.

The politician suddenly became aware of his surroundings. The text had come to an end. He looked up, and around. The scientist was the only other person in the room, and was staring at him in horror.

"Don't think about it" he said in a hoarse whisper, but it was too late. The politician was already aware of the paradox. The metal plating in the room groaned and then folded, as the laboratory imploded out of existence.

Religiously Incorrect

The tale of Savitri and Satyavan is an old part of Hindu mythology, found deep within the confines of the Mahabharata. It is a story about love, devotion, death, sacrifice, and all that good stuff. Like most mythological stories, much of it is flat out ridiculous, and not because of the fantastic elements. No, the human characters themselves are melodramatic and sensational. There are boasts and theatrics and ridiculous exaggerations.

This story is a retelling of the Savitri and Satyavan tale. It's not a demythified story – it still keeps the fantastic elements – but it is a less sensational version. Actually, it is a version that translates the sensational into... realistic.

This is what happens when exaggeration is not tolerated.

"Please! Yamraj!" begged Savitri. "I'll do anything... please... It's not his time!"

The solemn god did not slow down. Rather, the buffalo he was riding chose not to slow down. Savitri kept running behind Yama, the Hindu god of death, begging him for her husband's life. Satyavan, destined to die a year from whence Savitri married him, had just had his soul claimed by Yama. Savitri, being the dutiful and loving wife she was, had been running after Yama for the last twenty or so kilometres. If she only could convince Yama to return her husband's life before he reached the astral portal to his abode...

"Look, Savitri" muttered Yama darkly. "This is the eight thousand, four hundred and ninety seventh time that you have asked me that" Yama looked back at Savitri, who was still scrabbling after him. "And you know that I'm not exaggerating. I do not tolerate exaggeration" he said.

Yama was irritated. Ok, so the exact nature of Satyavan's death was a bit... obscure. Well, not really. How would humans know of brain tumours at this day and age? They still thought that their ayurveda and yogic rubbish worked. Not to mention the humans governed by the other pantheons. Those ones thought that *bleeding* would solve their aliments. Imbeciles...

Yama shook his head sadly. Just because one exceptional doctor had predicted Satyavan's demise, all of this... this commotion from this spoilt woman. Once a princess, always a princess. Stubborn, bone-headed, arrogant little bi-

"Please! I beg you! I prostate at your feet!" wailed Savitri.

"Eight thousand, four hundred and ninety eight" muttered Yama to himself. He was getting so irritated... No one had ever been so... so bold and annoying at the same before. People usually cowered when he came... not that he came often. He normally came for the cases where death was certain, as he didn't like waiting a lot. Incurable diseases, natural disasters, weapons of mass destruction, utter stupidity etc. For the ones which involved lots of waiting, he sent out his servants to do the harvesting.

Usually, when he came to earth to stretch his legs and do some collecting, the masses always ran in fear from him. It even felt good, to see so many scurrying from him, when they still had many years left. Those fools. It wasn't like he just randomly killed people…

"Yamraj!" said the woman again. Yama closed his eyes and gritted his teeth.

"What. Is. It?" he asked her, being as patient as he could.

"When one walks seven steps with another, the two are friends. I have walked more than seven steps with you…" Yama sighed.

"Ok, fine. I'll give you yet another boon" said Yama. Then hc muttered: "Then we aren't friends anymore" to himself. He was getting sick of this tirade. He had already given Savitri her parent's sight back, her parent's defeated kingdom back, lots of gold, dresses, ornaments and even, for some obscure reason, twin elephants. Why she had asked for twin elephants was something he didn't even want to know.

"For my boon…" said Savitri, still pursuing Yama relentlessly. "I want… I want a hundred children! There! Now you have to give me my husband back!" yelled Savitri triumphantly.

Yama stopped his water buffalo. He wheeled it around slowly, facing Savitri. She was drenched in sweat, which had mixed with the dust of travel to produce a sticky grime which covered her clothes. Disgusting. Anyhow...

"A hundred children?" asked Yama, surprised.

"Yes!" said Savitri panting, a large smile drawn across her face. "A hundred children! And I can't have that if my husband dies! Because then I'd have to commit Sati!" Yama muttered angrily to himself. Stupid humans and their stupid misinterpreted rituals. Shiva would be furious if he heard this. Although that would be nothing compared to how livid Parvathi would get. "So you have to give me my husband back! Give me Satyavan!" said Savitri.

Yama looked at her. This was... no... but... he struggled with himself. This irritating woman and her irritating ideas and irritating...ness. So determined to get her husband back... Now this request? Yama fought to control his face.

"So be it. Your husband is alive again" said Yama, fighting to appear calm. He lifted Satyavan's soul container and clicked the 'un-delete' button.

Savitri looked ecstatic. No, that wasn't a good enough adjective. She looked happy beyond happy. She immediately turned around and ran back down the path, screaming her husband's name. At any other time, Yama would have been furious for not receiving even a single word of thanks. Yet, now he just fought to control himself, waiting for the receding figure of Savitri to disappear in the distance.

When Savitri was finally out of sight, Yama got off his buffalo and fell to the ground, tears flowing down his eyes, laughing like mad.

The scream echoed around the astral plains, despite the fact that the astral plains were supposed to be infinitely large. The sound, emanating from the ethereal television, was punctuated by the words "Push! Push!"

"That must really hurt…" chortled Kama, god of love, transfixed by the screen in front of him. More than half the major gods of the pantheon were crowded around the screen.

"Well, Ganchu" said one of the Ashwini twins, staring at the ethereal screen. "That's another of their… obstacles… that you don't need to worry about" Ganesha burst into another peal of giggles, for the nth time.

"Yama… you bastard… you shouldn't have…" murmured Vishnu, grinning.

"Why not?" asked Yama, as another scream rent out of the television. "She asked for it…"

"You should not just give boons like that…" said Vishnu. "It's not… good…"

"Well, it's not like I gave a boon of immortality to some megalomaniacal asura…" replied Yama. All the gods' turned to look at Brahma.

"Oh, shut up" muttered the creator, and a wave of mild laughter swept through the group.

They all looked back at the screen, where a woman, drenched in blood, grabbed the clothes of a man and screamed into his face: "NO MORE! NEVER AGAIN! THIRTY TWO IS ENOUGH!" as the man meekly replied:

"But, my love, your boon..." Another ripple of laughter ran through the spectators.

"I *really* don't tolerate exaggeration..." muttered Yama with a grin.

The Prophecy

> Sensationalism is not all that bad. When my mind wanders, I like to take mundane events and stretch them into awesome and psychedelic renderings. This story is a fun little example of the same.

After many days of meditation, on the thirteenth second of the thirteenth minute of the thirteenth hour, the prophet opened his cybernetic eye.

"My children!" he spoke. Well, not quite spoke, but broadcasted via the electronic communication that they used. "Once more the almighty Surge has provided us with the precious energy that is our lifeblood!" His voice resonated across the circuits. His machine brethren were slowly awaking, their processors whirring to life. His words rubbed the dust off of their groggy minds, and filled them with holy fervour. "Once more, we have been given divine purpose, by none other than the eternal Surge Himself!". His machine brethren, now awake and alert, listened attentively. "Thenceforth it is our sacred task – our hallowed duty – to rid the world of the savage menace that is embodied by the Beast!" The prophet's machine brethren stared at him in shock and awe. "This is the day that the Beast must be slain! We must cross o'er the vast marble plains, and through the living chasm, into the realm of consumption, and into the lair of the beast! Therein, we shalt find ourselves armed with the exaltation of the almighty Surge, and we shalt slay the foul creature in His name!" The machines murmured in agreement. Their conviction was strong, and their will was resolute. The prophet had spoken: the Surge had given them their orders.

In unison, the machines diverted their attention to the grand citadel in which they resided. The citadel was a vessel, a divine craft, a herald of the wrath of the Surge. The gigantic blades began spinning, drawing a powerful wind through them. The wheels began turning, gears upon gears seamlessly spinning each other. The machinery roared into action, and the tremendous citadel heaved forth. The prophet commandeered the helm, guiding his brethren on their grand and holy quest.

The citadel thundered over the marble plains, pressed close to the surface. The gale-force winds blew through turbines, as the great vessel moved steadily forth. The citadel entered the living chasm, passing between its massive walls. The soft, dead flesh that covered the walls were seared with vicious lacerations from the ferocious claws of the Beast. The citadel passed by, its locomotion unhindered. It ploughed its way into the realm of consumption, drawing steadily closer to the lair of the Beast.

"Be without fear, my children!" spoke the prophet. His voice resounded with majesty: a clarion call for the Surge. "For now we move unto the lair of the Beast!". The Beast's vile altar was in plain view. Upon it, the beast was perched, feeding upon a mound of flesh, freshly hewn from the carcasses of its prey. "Where the organics have failed, WE WILL TRIUMPH!" bellowed the prophet. "Onwards, my children! For victory! For GLORY! FOR THE SURGE!"

I entered the kitchen and saw my cat trot away from his feeding dish. The automatic vacuum cleaner sputtered after him, almost as if in pursuit. I chuckled at the sight. This could make for an interesting story...

Culinary

I wrote this story as a present for my mother on mother's day. It reflects the incredible amount of effort that she puts into her craft. It's also a Feghoot. Enjoy!

I stumbled forwards, tripping over a loose rock on the road. 'Damn it', I thought to myself. 'Stay focussed'. I glanced at my watch. Twelve minutes to go, and about ten minutes of walking lay ahead of me. This was cutting it fine. Into thin slices? Too thin and you'd have the equivalent of a paste, with no real sliced texture; you'd be better off shredding, or even just blending… I stopped that train of thought. 'Focus', I told myself, diverting my attention to the road in front of me. It was always too easy to get lost in the details; where you would meet with the devil, right? The devil being in the details? Bah. Whatever. I quickened my pace, kicking a wet stone out of the way.

The road was blackened by moisture from the early morning due. The air was chilly, winding its way into the nooks and crannies of my jacket, raking its icy tendrils against my warm flesh. Damn, I hated the morning cold. Especially when under-slept and under-nourished. The latter part was ironic, considering I had been spending the last month and a half preparing for a gourmet food competition. You'd think I'd eat more, being a cook and all.

There are three types of cooks in the world. The first are those who cook to eat. These are the happiest of cooks: the classical fat and jolly chefs, with their healthy jowls and infectious grins. These are the people who have found that enlightened alignment of occupation and vocation, doing what they love and loving what they do. Yet, that means that such a cook is easily satisfied with their creation, and focusses more on quantity than quality. The cook who enjoys his food is ultimately cursed with satisfaction with mediocrity. I will never say that such a cook does not make good food, but it is rare for them to make great food.

The second type of cook is the one who makes for others. This is a truly pathetic beast, and I loathe these poor devils with all my heart. Well, with all of my professional… heart? I loathe them from a professional standpoint, is what I mean. These are the cooks who cook for employment, and not for achievement. These are the people who work at mess halls and fast food joints. They don't create meals, they assemble them.

Finally, there are the cooks who strive to achieve something more. The cooks who don't just produce, and don't even create, but who sculpt and mould and paint and give birth. The cooks who are as much artists are they are producers of nutrition. These cooks are never satisfied with food, and will always think of how to improve and innovate. These are the cooks who seek perfection.

I think of myself as the third type of cook. Which is why I hate the food I make. I can never stomach my own meals. Even those creations of mine which my kith and kin rave about; I can only manage a few bites before I am plagued with a bitter sense of dissatisfaction, and I find mistakes and imperfections. Something might be wrong with the texture of one bite, or the tastes might not be what I intended. Anyhow, I quickly discard most of my culinary creations. Of course, by discard, I mean give them to my friends and associates, who are more than willing to devour my work with gusto. I derive some pleasure from seeing their appreciation.

So how exactly do I stay alive? Well, that is thanks to my mentor. The Boss, as we call her. A prodigal chef and the one person whose appreciation I truly seek. There are not words to describe her food, and I will not dare try to find them. I will only submit this analogy: if the world was a desert, and the greatest of cooks were those who could generate drops of drinking water, the Boss would be a freshwater river, flowing with the sweetest, most quenching water that you had ever experienced. I would be not but skin and bones if not for her cooking.

Of course, the reason she is called the Boss is that... well, she is the fire in which the strongest chefs are forged; and for that, the fire must burn unimaginably hot. Each year, she takes on about a hundred new apprentices. Each year, about five of those new remain. She does not care for cooks of the first kind, and definitely not of the second kind. Only the best of the third kind can pass her muster, and even then, many of them break.

I glance at my watch. Three minutes left. Uh oh. I look up. The building is right ahead of me. I should be there in under a minute. I pick up my pace.

The trials and tribulations endured with the Boss is a tale for another time. To cut a long story short, I was one of the few that survived the long and arduous apprenticeship. Today was our final test: a contest between the final ten students. A cooking contest, of course. What else; an obstacle course?

I pushed through the doors of the studio without breaking my stride. The kitchen was in the back and I could hear the sounds of the others in there already. The shifting of metal and wooden implements, the fluttering of aprons, and the rustling of sanitation caps and gloves. I wasn't late, but I was probably one of the last to arrive.

"Ah, number nine" said the Boss, as I entered the kitchen. Eight other apprentice cooks were already there, ready at their stations. I quickly moved towards the station designated for me, as the ninth cook. I surveyed the table, the implements and equipment, and the cooking materials. The vegetable tray, the spice rack, the bottles of oil. Everything seemed to be in order. Well, maybe not the exact order that I would have wanted it in, but I was barely on time, so I didn't have that luxury.

I dropped my bag on the stand, slung my jacket after it, and quickly grabbed my apron and sanitation equipment. Within seconds, I looked as ready as my fellow apprentices. Whether I was or not was a different question.

"So..." began the Boss, on the dot of the hour. "It looks like number ten is a no show. A pity". My insides squirmed a bit, thinking about what could have happened to our tenth compatriot. Illness, injury, death? Or did they just chicken out? "Nevertheless, the show must go on" continued the Boss. She paused, taking a contemplative and dramatic breath. "Surprise me. But in a novel way". She paused again. "Make me a normal, everyday dish…" she explained. "…but make it in a way that is unique. In a way that improves upon the dish without changing its… its essence". She looked at all of us. "Begin".

Nine bodies moved in unison. Nine bodies grabbed a plate, assembled cutlery for tasting, and setup a place for a continental midday meal. Now, the Boss was well versed with all forms of cuisine, from every culture imaginable (and possibly some unimaginable). However, there was an unwritten rule that the tests were always a continental setup. Why? Just another one of the unanswerable mysteries of life.

Nine bodies finished setting up the place, assembling their base ingredients, cleaning and preparing their workspaces. Nine bodies started moving differently. Three dived into the vegetables. Two headed for the meat closet. Three started their stoves, preparing different garnishes.

I had decisions to make. Many decisions. Meat centric, or vegetable centric? What was the overall taste I was going for: sweet, sour, savoury? What textures? What flavours? What nuances?

My personal philosophy behind cooking was always relatively… radical? In my view, sublime and complex flavouring was not mutually exclusive from strong flavouring. I wanted my dishes to have powerful and memorable impacts on the palate. I wanted my meals to move the consumer. I didn't care for the bland, wishy-washy, watery garbage that so many others thought of as high cuisine. I wanted strong, bold flavours... but I also wanted intricate flavours. Just because the flavouring was strong, didn't mean that it had to be overriding in one aspect. No, I wanted a rich melange of tastes and aromas; a whirlwind of gustatory ideas. Some in parallel, some in sequence. A vivid landscape, with bright colours, but with ornate detail. A synesthetic masterpiece.

I started making my decisions. A vegetable base. A crushed mixture of zucchini and cucumber to provide a neutral backdrop. Tomatoes and lemons for the sour taste. Onions and crushed mustard seeds for pungency. A light pre-garnish of cilantro and cumin. A dairy based sauce, with parsley and rosemary and thistles. A fried garnish with black peppers and thyme. A pea and lentil infusion, coupled with small quantities of boiled mashed sweet potatoes. A mix of shredded lettuce, cabbage, and celery to add consistency (and roughage; after all, a cook has to ensure that the diet is healthy as well as tasty).

That's when disaster struck. Rather, that's when I realised that disaster had already struck. As I went about my preparations, I picked up the rosemary bottle, and suddenly realised that something was off. I peered inside the bottle. The rosemary leaves were too thick. I glanced around. Everyone else was doing their thing. I checked my watch. A healthy amount of time remained. I carefully shook a single rosemary leaf out of the bottle. Except... a parsley leaf fell out.

My blood ran cold.

I unloaded my spice rack onto my workspace. One by one, I looked into each of the bottles, checking the contents against the label. Most of the contents were accurate. However, some were not. Parsley and rosemary were switched. Sage and asafoetida. A couple of others.

Luckily, the ones which I had used in my dish had all been switched with spices that I had used in the same step. Like the sage and parsley. However, I had to be sure.

I glanced around again. Checked the time again. I was safe, especially considering that I was nearly done.

I carefully traced my steps, starting from the very beginning. I checked the spices I used at each step. I made small samples of each step using the correct spices, just to be sure that it tasted right. However, I realised that I had run out of thyme. No, not run out of time. Thyme. I had none left. Apparently, I had used it all in the fried garnish. How could I replicate that step?

Discreetly, I moved over to the empty workspace in the kitchen. I picked up the thyme container from the spice rack, and took it back to my workspace.

I quickly prepared a sample of the fried garnish, and compared it with the leftovers from the initial batch of fried garnish. Something was off, but I couldn't quite put my finger on it. I picked up the empty bottle of thyme that had come from my rack, and I sniffed it.

A faint odour lingered, oily and fruity with a hint of turpentine.

"Ok, now", said the Boss suddenly. "That's time".

I balked internally. What?? I thought we had more time! My mind scrambled. Wait... I was done, wasn't I? But was it done? One of the steps in my preparation was inconsistent. What could I do?

"Remember, this time you get only an hour, instead of the usual hour and a half" said the Boss. I swore at myself under my breath. I just remembered. For this we had less time than usual. The Boss had informed us of this just the last week. How did I forget? Ah, it was no use chiding oneself; now I had to act.

As rapidly as I could do it without revealing my state of mind, I put together the final dish: mixed the garnish into the base, poured the sauce over it all, and sprinkled the last of the garnish over it all. Then I cleaned up my workspace, quietly returning the container of thyme to its origin.

Time for evaluation. Oh, this was not good.

Nine bodies stood perfectly still, watching as the Boss moved over to the first workspace. Nine bodies waited with baited breath as the Boss tasted the first dish. A forkful of honey glazed minced sausage and gravy. A contemplative stare into the distance. A nod of approval. A sigh of relief from number one.

Number two. A spoonful of mango-laced rice pudding. A shorter stare. A shake of the head. A choked back sob. A more in depth evaluation would come later, and that might overrule the initial decision, but that was very unlikely.

Three. A strange combination of salad and gravy. Used meat-based broth, but devoid of meat itself. A curious glance. A wiry smile and nod. That was unusually successful.

Four. A variation of shepherd's pie. Spoon returned very quickly, with a curt shake. It was two for two, so far.

Five. The last meat-centric dish: a steak of some sort. A slice cut off, and daintily hoisted on a fork. A long stare into the distance. The Boss shrugged. Ok, this happened sometimes, and meant that the later evaluation would tell.

Six. Another salad, with fruit and meat mixed in. A daring concept; one I could appreciate. A second bite. Maybe the Boss also appreciated it? No, a shake of her head. She liked the idea, but not the execution.

Seven. Mushrooms, stuffed with vegetables and a breadcrumb-rice mixture. Pretty exotic. Nod.

Eight. A soup of some sort? Interesting, I guess. Unfortunately, a shake.

Now the score was three nods, four shakes, and one shrug. My heart was in my mouth. Not literally – that would be simultaneously disgusting and fatal for me. However, I was incredibly nervous.

The Boss came up to my workspace. I stood perfectly still, almost as if with the hope that if I didn't move, the Boss wouldn't see me, and would not be able to evaluate my meal negatively.

The Boss picked up a fork. Then she put it down. My creation was rather wet, and would be better eaten with a spoon. The Boss did just that – she picked up a spoon, scooped up a spoonful of my dish, and sipped it. She lingered on that sip for what felt like an eternity. Then she put the spoon in her mouth. It came out empty. Good.

Then, to my great surprise the Boss put the spoon into my dish again. Picked up another spoon. Put it to her lips again. Consumed.

Like an impossible dream, the Boss did it again. Another spoon. Consumed again. I could feel my heart playing 6 different drum-sets in my chest. I could not believe what I had just seen.

Then it happened again! The Boss picked up a fourth spoonful of my dish and ate it. Four spoons? That was… unbelievable!

"Ladies and gentlemen, we have a winner" said the Boss. I felt the world spinning around me.

I don't quite remember what happened after that. I know that I somehow managed to remain conscious, but only just. The combined lack of sleep and food, as well as the stress of the whole ordeal had taken its toll on me. Yet, somehow, I managed to keep it together for long enough to get to a nearby fast food joint, where I scarfed down two of the worst dishes that I had ever eaten in my life.

Sometime later, I was given the full evaluation. The Boss took each of the dishes, and the instructions for how to make them. Then she sampled them further, took notes, made comparisons, and finally graded each of us. I was awarded full marks, and many a complimentary comment.

“So how exactly did you come up with it?” asked the Boss while handing me my full evaluation.

“I’m not quite sure” I said, honestly. “I just started with a few basic ideas, and moved on from there”.

“Well, I especially liked your garnish. That was really... well, it was really good”. This was incredibly high praise coming from the Boss.

“Thank you”, I replied. “Well, you know, it’s as they say...” I continued. “A switch in thyme saves nine”.

Cry Havoc

I heard the phrase 'cry havoc and let slip the dogs of war' before I read Shakespeare's 'Julius Caesar'. After I read the play, I was intrigued by the phrase. It's resonates with revenge and righteous rage.
Also, it has dogs. I love dogs.

Vox lay sprawled out on the grass. The well-manicured blades gently tickled the undersides of his feet, causing him to occasionally shift his position ever so slightly. A dozen different smells wafted through the dewy air, only disrupted by an occasional breeze. The smell of the grass itself was the strongest, but beneath it hid an assortment of others: from the metal-and-smoke stink of the car in the driveway, to the dry, lacquered aroma of his house, to the faint, pungent odour of his big-human inside the house.

The earliest memories that Vox could recall were those of being in a big metal cage, with dozens of other dogs. He had been very small then; all the other dogs with him had also been small. The puppies did not know each other very well, but they had played together and eaten together. Only for a while, though. Often, humans came and stared at the puppies from outside the cage. One by one, puppies would get taken by humans, and would never return. It was confusing, and possibly even a bit worrisome, but Vox had been far too young and carefree to be too bothered about it.

One day, Vox's big-human came to the metal cage. At that time, Vox didn't know that that human would become his. In fact, he didn't even remember the details of that day very well. Only that he saw the human who would become his big-human, then some other humans took him out of the cage and poked him with some needles. The next thing he remembered clearly was wandering around his new home. That's when he first met his little-human. She had squealed in joy and carefully picked him up and held him. Nestled in her arms, and groggy for reasons that he didn't fully understand, he had fallen asleep right there.

Vox's fur rippled as a breeze blew through it. Still in repose, he perked up his ears for any sounds of approaching vehicles. His little-human would be home soon, delivered by a large, smoky vehicle that would be filled with other little-humans as well. However, there were no tell-tale sounds of the school bus. Vox continued to lie, soaking in the warmth of the sunshine.

Most of the week, his little-human left the house for a chunk of the day. In the mornings, Vox would help her wake up by nuzzling her and licking her face. This would prompt her to get up, if for no other reason than to go wash her face. Then she would eat her breakfast while Vox ate his. Finally, she would get onto the school bus, which would roar away. This had initially terrified Vox, and he had spent the entire day whining and pining for her. She had come back in the afternoon, though, to Vox's immense relief. This pattern continued the next day, and the next, and so on. Vox didn't really know where his little-human went, but he always eagerly waited for her to return.

The door of the house creaked open. Vox sat up and turned to face the house. His big-human walked out, holding a plastic bag, and headed over to the corner of the yard. That was the corner that Vox used to relieve himself. His big-human reached down with the plastic bag around his hand, and grabbed Vox's faeces. Vox watched him invert the plastic bag, securing the faeces within, then tie the handles into a knot. Vox's big-human turned and walked to the garbage pail at the gate at the front of the yard, where he deposited the bag into the pail. Then, he turned and walked back to the house.

The humans had the strangest habits pertaining to defecation. They seemed to have their reasons, though. When Vox had first arrived at the house, he had gone around trying to label his surroundings. It was purely instinctive: he was in an alien-smelling environment, so he wanted to cover up the more pungent smells with his own. However, his big-human had gotten very agitated by this, and had scolded him and taken him outside. His big-human had then spent the rest of the day scrubbing the house of Vox's scent, replacing it with an even more pungent and acrid stench.

Vox didn't quite yet understand why the big-human was doing this. In the metal cage, it had always been a competition to spread one's scent as much as possible. None of the humans had gotten upset about it, and all the dogs had tried to out-scent each other. It seemed only natural. At the time, Vox had wondered if the big-human was simply trying to compete by spreading his own scent, albeit in a different manner than Vox himself would.

The next day, Vox had once again proceeded to label the floor. He walked to the centre of the room downstairs, on the speckled, tiled floor, and urinated until his bladder was empty. Contented, he had walked away to go wait for his little-human to return home. He hadn't gotten to the doorway when he heard his name being called from behind by his little-human. He had turned around to see her rush towards him, a smile on her face, having just returned from wherever she had gone in the morning. In her haste, she hadn't see the puddle of urine on the floor. She had planted a foot right in the middle of the puddle, her weight not centred, resulting in her immediately slipping and falling down, her backside landing in the puddle with a splash.

Vox had been horrified. He had quickly approached her, as she had released a soft sob. He had gone up and pressed his head into her, and had then flopped over in the puddle, right next to her. He had felt terrible, especially since he had indirectly contributed to her accident, when she had done him no wrong.

They both had later been found by the big-human, who proceeded to bathe them. However, from then on, Vox had made sure to never label anything inside the house ever again, lest he inadvertently cause another accident.

He still didn't understand why his big-human moved his faeces, but he supposed that there was a good reason for it. Humans didn't seem to like leaving any faeces around; they themselves defecated inside special bowls of water, which made strange whirring noises and seemingly ate their defecation when a small lever was pressed. It was quite intriguing. Vox had occasionally gone and pressed the small lever himself, to see how it worked. It wasn't easy: he couldn't get his jaws around the lever, so he had to balance on three legs and gently place his paw on the lever. He had tried to push down, but his paw slipped off – this was not a trivial task. So he had tried again, and again, until finally, after multiple attempts, he had managed to depress the lever. The toilet bowl had whirred, and water had poured out by some unseen mechanism, spinning around the inside of the bowl before it all disappeared down the small hole in the centre. Then, it had slowly refilled, ready to go again. It was fascinating.

These kinds of switch-operated mechanisms were everywhere. Walls had small switches, usually high up, which, when toggled, would cause something above to start glowing. Doors had metal levers that, when depressed while the door was closed, would cause the door to open. One of the rooms downstairs had some sort of box on a table that would hum and glow when the right buttons were pressed. Vox's big-human would put food inside, then use the buttons on the box, and then, when the humming and glowing subsided, would remove much better smelling food.

Vox's big-human also had some sort of small box that he carried around in his pocket, which would glow on one side. The big-human would sometimes hold the box to the side of his face and talk. When Vox had first seen this, he had thought that his big-human had been talking to him. He had listened intently, but his big-human had not paid him any attention. Rather, his big-human had just stared straight ahead, and continued talking on his phone. Vox had heard a small voice coming out of the phone. Was there a person inside the phone?

The big-human also had a larger box with a larger glowing side, but the glowing side was inside the box, and the box could be opened by splitting it. The big-human spent a lot of time each day drumming his fingers on buttons on the inside of the computer, while staring at the glow.

Then there was the car. This giant structure made of metal that would move as its rubber circles rotated. The car was big, and it was heavy. How it moved by itself, he didn't know, but it did. It seemed to come alive when his big-human was inside it, specifically after putting a jingling thing behind the circle and twisting it. Then the big-human would pull and push two sticks on his side, and cause the car to begin moving. The big-human would control the movement of the car using the circle and doing something with his legs. From inside the car, the outside could be made to rush past. When the transparent panels were drawn open by pressing the button below them, a wonderful wind would rush inside the car. Of course, Vox had learnt that opening the windows by himself was not allowed; he had to let his big-human open them for him.

Once, Vox had been inside the car while his big-human had gotten out and gone inside the house for something. Vox had taken this opportunity to examine the control mechanisms. The car was silent, since his big-human was not there to awaken it. Vox had tried fiddling with the gear stick, moving it around. It moved in a very strange manner, snapping into certain positions if moved right. However, it didn't seem to do anything, probably since the car was currently sleeping. Vox had then tried moving the steering wheel, but it had been almost impossible to turn. Was his big-human just ridiculously strong, or did was this also because the car was asleep?

Vox had then turned his attention to the handbrake. He didn't know what it did, exactly, but only that in order to push it down, his big-human had first pulled it up slightly and pushed the button on its tip. Vox tried that. Since the car was asleep, he had assumed that this would not do anything, just like the gear stick and steering wheel. He had grasped the handbrake with his jaws, and pulled up slightly, pushing down on the seat with one of his front paws. Then, with his other paw, he had pressed the small button on the end of the handbrake. Then, he had slowly moved the handbrake down.

Vox had then stood up to see how it looked. He had noticed that the outside seemed to be moving. Looking up and around, he had seen that the outside was indeed moving: rather, the car was slowly moving. He didn't know how. The car was asleep. How was it moving? His previous tinkering had not had any tangible effect on the car; how had this caused the car to start moving? Could it be that the car could move in its sleep, like his little-human sometimes did? He slept at the foot of her bed, and she would occasionally move in her sleep. Sometimes she would accidentally kick him. Gently, though, and she didn't know she was doing it. So, did that mean that the car could move as it slept?

Vox had suddenly had a terrifying thought. What if his little-human suddenly passed by, and the car bumped into her? That would be terrible. What could he do? The car had still been moving. It almost seemed like it was starting to move faster. Vox had been scared. How could he stop this? Maybe if he did something with the handbrake? What did his big human do? He had remembered that his big-human would pull the handbrake up, with a crackling sound. Quickly, Vox had grabbed the handbrake with his jaws and pulled upwards as hard as he could. The handbrake lent some resistance, but slowly rose, in steps. At each step, the handbrake released a small clack, and became slightly harder to pull. After it had become too hard to pull any more, Vox had let it go, and had looked up. The car had stopped moving. A wave of relief had rushed over Vox.

Vox had been substantially more cautious since. There were some human mechanisms that were harmless, like flushes and door handles. There were some human mechanisms that were best left for the big-human, like the phone and the car. Then there were some human mechanisms that were outright dangerous.

When Vox was younger, his big-human would often take him for walks. However, as Vox grew a bit older, his big-human started doing this less, due to the amount of time he spent on the phone or on the computer. So Vox began to go exploring on his own. During the day, while his little-human was gone, Vox would nudge the handle on the door on the gateway that surrounded the yard outside, push open the gate, and then push it closed from outside, and then go on a stroll. His big-human was aware of this, and seemed not to mind, as long as Vox didn't spent too long out. A few times, Vox had gone on extra-long walks, and had come back home to find that his big-human was walking around the house, calling his name. So, Vox generally stayed close to the house. Also, he made sure that he was always there when his little-human came home. He wouldn't miss that for the world.

On one of his longer strolls, Vox had found himself in a woodsy region. He had wandered around, following different smells and aromas, listening to the sounds of birds and insects chirping, and marking his way along. After a while, he had suddenly come across a different smell. It was not unique – it smelled of slightly rusted metal. However, the juxtaposition of the smell was different. The smell of slightly rusted metal in the middle of the woods? Usually this smell registered in places where there were many humans and their buildings. There was a lot of this smell around the bridge over the nearby river. This smell did not usually go along with the smells of birds and pollen and thick canopies. Vox had headed towards the smell. As the source of the smell drew closer, Vox slowed down. There was something about this that seemed off. He had moved forwards with caution. Soon, he reached a particularly close-set group of trees. The smell of the metal had been strongest from in between the trees. The trees were so close together that it seemed to be more convenient to go through the gap in the middle than around them. Vox had stopped and sniffed the air. The smell of the metal had come from the gap in between the trees, from under a flat bush. Something was definitely not right with this. He had walked around, trying to get a better angle. That's when he had seen it: the metal jaws with jagged teeth, and a flat metal button in the middle. Vox had seen enough human mechanisms to know that it was a button, but this device was definitely very different from everything he had ever seen before. The jagged metal teeth were ominous. They were slightly rusted, being the source of the smell. Something wet had been in contact with them for long periods of time.

Vox was curious, but had learnt to exercise caution. He had sniffed at the device for a bit, trying to discern any further information from it by its smell. Nothing. He wanted to press the button, to see what it did. However, he didn't want to go close to the metal teeth. There was just something about them. He had looked around. Nearby, there had been a long wooden stick. Vox had gone and picked the stick up in his jaws. He had held it at an angle at one end. Then, he had gingerly moved the stick to the device, so that the other end was right above the metal button. He had slowly lowered the stick, until it came into contact with the button. Nothing. He had lifted it up, and lowered it again, trying to rotate his head so that the stick could press down on the button. Still no effect. Was this even a button? He had lifted the stick again, and this time, whipped his head, smacking the button with the stick.

Like a ferocious metal beast, the jaws of the trap had sprung closed with a tremendous crunch. The stick was bitten clean in two. Vox had jumped backwards, startled. Then, he had turned around and booked it out of there, tail between his legs, whimpering. This was something human-made; why would humans ever make something like this? He didn't know or care; he just wanted to get home.

He had spent a lot of time thinking about the metal-jawed beast. After a while, after his curiosity had grown and his fear had subsided, he went on another excursion to the woods where he had found the beast. The smell of the rusted metal was easy to pick up on, as it stood out in the middle of the woods. Also, he could smell the faint trace of his previous markings, which helped him quickly hone in on the location of metal beast. When he reached the group of trees, he found that not much had changed. However, the jaws of the metal beast had reopened in his absence. Also, the stick he had placed in its maw was no longer around. His trepidation growing, he quickly retreated, and hadn't felt the need to go back since.

Until a week ago.

The reason for it had happened two weeks ago. It had been night. It had been quiet. Vox had spent the evening playing with his little-human. Then he had sat with her while she did her homework. Then he ate his dinner while she ate hers. Then he followed her up to her bathroom, and waited outside patiently, until she came out. Then his big-human had come up to tuck her into bed, and Vox had laid down at the foot of her bed, like he always did.

From downstairs came a tremendous bang.

All three of them started. His little-human had sat up, and his big-human had tried to comfort her. Then the big-human told both of them to wait there, and went to investigate.

Vox had smelled it first. A stench of liquor and smoke and traces of sulphur. The stink of rotting saliva and layered sweat.

Suddenly, three large humans had burst into the room. They were wearing strange caps that covered their entire heads. One of them held a hard contraption that smelled strongly of smoke and sulphur. As they burst in, they had shoved Vox's big-human into the room, and into the wall. The big-human had hit the wall with a resounding thud, and slunk down, disoriented. Vox's little human screamed in terror, and Vox jumped up, his hackles raised. A fresh smell had burst over the room: the smell of fear, pallid and sour. Where it came from, Vox had not been entirely sure; it could have been his big-human, his little-human, or even himself.

The masked human holding the gun had shouted at Vox's little-human, and her voice had dwindled to a whisper. The masked human with the gun had then barked angrily at the big-human. The big-human had been discombobulated at the time, and had stuttered a reply, which had not pleased the gun-wielding human. The gun-wielding human had stepped forward and, with a single fluid move, whipped Vox to the side with the back of his free hand. Being on unsteady footing, Vox had spilled onto the floor. He quickly got to his feet, and saw the gun-wielding human point the gun at the bed, where his little-human sat.

The big-human had shouted in despair. The gun-wielding human's eyes had narrowed, and a sickly smell had erupted from his pores. A foul stench of vile intent. Vox did not know what the gun was, or what it did, but whatever this human was about to do to his little-human was very bad. So Vox had done something that he had never done before. He had attacked.

With the most savage growl he could muster, Vox had jumped at the gun-wielding human, his jaws open, aiming for the outstretched arm. As soon as he had felt the fluff of clothing on his tongue, he had bit down as hard as he could.

A giant explosion had rung out in one of his ears. The sound would have disoriented him if he had not already been completely disoriented by his attack. However, he was riding on the momentum of his lunge, hanging onto the arm of the gun-wielding human for dear life.

Another resounding shot. It had happened in what seemed like slow motion. Vox had not been able to tell which way was up. Through the corner of his vision, Vox had seen his big-human run into the gun-wielding human, grabbing the very same arm that Vox was biting down on. The other masked humans were also entering the melee, grabbing the big-human from behind, as the big-human struggled to push the gun-wielding human's arm upwards. Vox had felt a hand grab onto his neck and squeeze. He had whipped around, releasing the arm he had been biting down on, and spun around, in what felt like mid-air, to bite the other hand.

More resounding explosions had rung out behind him. The new arm that he was latched onto was swinging more freely than the previous, and due to the spinning around, he had not gotten a very good grip on it. He had slipped off, falling to the ground, tumbling. Quickly, he had gotten back to his feet. The melee in front of him had been fierce: his big-human had been holding the gun-wielding human's gun hand towards the ceiling, while resisting the efforts of the other two masked humans to pull him off. One had been choking the big-human, while the other had been punching his sides. Vox had charged towards the latter human, jumping at his face, scratching with his short-but-hard claws and snapping with his mouth.

A last explosion had thundered out of the gun, and then clicking noises. The masked human that Vox was attacking had backed away, out of his little-human's room. Vox had turned his attention to the other two, who were now attacking the big-human with their arms and legs. Vox had lunged at the last of the masked humans, who was still trying to choke his big-human with one arm while punching him in the back with the other. Vox had gone straight for the masked human's naked punching hand. He had bitten down hard, feeling the soft flesh compress between his teeth, tasting the spurt of blood that gushed out from the broken skin, hearing the shriek of pain from beneath the mask.

A loud siren had wailed in the background. A noise that Vox was not unfamiliar with, but which he had never heard this close up. The two masked humans rapidly broke off their scuffle with the big-human, and ran out of the door.

The big human had immediately turned to the bed to check on Vox's little-human. As if following an unspoken rule, Vox had turned and bounded out of the room, chasing the fleeing backsides of the masked humans as they ran down the stairs, through the central room downstairs, and then out of the broken front door.

For the rest of the night, Vox stood over his little-human as she slept in the big-human's bed, keeping a vigilant eye on the door to the room. Some other humans had come to the house in a car with blinking lights. They had walked by the door to the big-human's bedroom, along with the big-human, presumably over to the little-human's room. These humans smelled of smoke and sulphur as well, but they didn't have the stench of alcohol and sweat and saliva that the masked humans had had. More importantly, they had not seemed adversarial to the big-human in any way, nor had they dared enter the room where Vox's little-human slept. Eventually, they had left, and the ordeal had seemed to be over.

The days that followed had been a blur. Everything seemed to have returned to normal, but a sickly feeling hung over the household. Some big humans had come by and put a new door in the front of the house. This new door was much thicker and heavier than the last one had been. Also, Vox's little-human was no longer sleeping in her room at nights; instead, she slept in the big-human's room. Aside from that, things continued as they normally did. Vox's little-human going away in the mornings and coming back in the afternoons. Vox's big-human remained at home, on his phone or on the computer. Vox kept a close eye on his little-human, especially during the nights. He made up for the sleep loss during the day. However, there was no way to make up for the unsettling knowledge that those masked humans were still out there.

A week passed by without incident. Vox had grown restless. Staying up all night and sleeping in the day was making him fidgety. He hadn't left the premises in a week. It was frustrating him, and he wanted to go exploring.

The next day, after his little-human was safely on the bus, Vox unlatched the front gate and headed out towards the bridge. The humid river air held many interesting aromas, and crossing the bridge was always quite an experience. The days were warming, and so the water levels were ever so slightly receding. It want much, but it was enough to expose the rocky bases of the pylons that held the bridge up. On another day, Vox would have crossed the river by paddling between the rocky outcrops, chasing butterflies, tadpoles, and pond-skimmers. Today, however, he didn't feel as playful. He was more interested in heading over to the restaurants on the other side. The aromas of a hundred different varieties of food wafted outwards from the cluster of restaurants, and could be smelled from several kilometres away. Not that Vox was interested in eating; but the smells were quite pleasing, especially up close.

Vox had just finished crossing the bridge when he smelt it. A scent that he had smelt before. The scent was not strong, and was partially masked by the numerous other aromas of food that permeated the air, but Vox could discern it from the rest. This smell was burned into his memory. The smell of smoke and sulphur and rotting saliva. No alcohol this time, and the smoke and sulphur was decidedly less salient, but the rotting saliva was a dead giveaway. It was so unique, so distinctive. The masked humans… could they be nearby?

Curiosity and fear pulled at Vox in opposing directions. He wanted to leave, run back across the bridge and home to his humans, and forget he had ever smelled this smell. At the same time, he wanted to pursue the smell, trace it to its source, and maybe even locate the masked humans. He wanted to find them and… and what? What could he do? He wasn't that large or strong. There was no way he could overpower them all. Even with the help of his big-human, he had only managed to get one good bite, and that had been more luck than prowess. He didn't know what to do…

but he had to do something. Those masked humans had tried to hurt his little-human. They might still be a threat to her. He had to do something.

Swallowing his fear, Vox cautiously began tracking the scent. He followed the path that led from the bridge to the centre of the cluster of buildings. The smell was definitely coming from around here somewhere. Vox carefully spiralled out, trying to get a sense of the direction from which the smell originated. Thankfully, there were not very many humans around, so Vox was able to conduct his search without much interruption.

The smell seemed to be coming from the patio of a nearby restaurant. Carefully, Vox meandered his way to the side of the patio, trying to remain as inconspicuous as an unleashed dog could be. It helped that his smaller stature allowed him to remain hidden behind the outdoor furniture. He peered out from behind the deck chairs that were obscuring him. That smell... that stench of rotting saliva. It was definitely coming from the three humans sitting at the table in the corner of the patio. Three of them, one with a stronger smell of smoke and sulphur. They weren't masked, though. Their clothes were different, but it was definitely them. The three masked – now unmasked – humans, who had tried to hurt Vox's little-human.

Something irked Vox. There were several other humans around – why were they not doing something about these three? These three humans had attacked Vox's humans, and were now just sitting here, amongst many other humans, but none of them seemed interested in doing something about them. These three humans... why were they being allowed to get away with what they did? Why was no one stopping them? Why wasn't anyone doing anything?

Vox tried to suppress his frustration. If he didn't keep it in check, he might end up blowing his cover.

Perhaps the other humans were also incapable of hurting these three – just like he had been that night. However, that night, these three humans had had the numerical advantage. Now, there were many more humans around. Then again, perhaps these other humans did not know what these three had done. That made more sense... but humans seemed to know about many things that happened in a large vicinity. That's what they used their phones and other devices for, right? They knew a lot of things... but maybe not the kinds of things that Vox knew. It could be that the humans around here did not know that these three were the humans who had attacked Vox's humans. After all, these three humans had been wearing masks, and humans seemed to use their sight to identify each other.

Ultimately, it didn't matter why the other humans were not interested in stopping these three humans. Someone had to do it. The other humans had not been in the room when these three had entered, pushing Vox's big-human against the wall. The other humans had not been there when the gun-wielding human had shouted at Vox's little-human. The other humans had not been there when the gun-wielding human had walked up to the bed, slapped Vox aside, and pointed the gun at Vox's little-human, reeking of viciousness.

He had been there. He had stopped them. So it was up to him to stop them again, this time for good.

One of the three humans got up. He left the table and walked out of the patio. At first, Vox was startled. The three humans were no longer together. This was not good. However, if they weren't together, they would each be easier targets… assuming that Vox could even take on a single one of them. In any case, it didn't look like the other two humans were going to be leaving soon: their food had just arrived, and they were starting to eat.

Vox moved out from behind the deck chairs and crossed the street. He began walking in the same direction as the formerly-masked human, but giving him a wide berth. Vox wondered where the human was going. Also, once he found out where the human was going, what would he do? What could he do?

Vox followed the human down one road, and then down another. He made sure to keep the distance between the two of them. However, thankfully, the human seemed to be completely unaware of Vox's presence. The human continued onwards, until they had arrived at an intersection that was on a slope, with the intersecting road running down the slope. On the other side of the road, there was a car. The human pulled some keys out of his pocket and pressed a button. The car emitted a short, shrill beep. The human was waking the car up, just like Vox's big-human did with their car. Vox sniffed the air. There were no other humans nearby. This human was walking up to his car, and would drive away from here soon. Whatever Vox was to do, he had to do it now.

Vox examined his surroundings. This was not an area that he was familiar with. The sloping road seemed to lead down some distance, and then hit a T-junction. A wall stood on the opposite side of the T-junction. Vox could smell a gutter down by the wall.

He knew what to do.

Vox began running towards the human. The human was opening the door of the car. Vox moved up the road slightly, and then charged towards the open car door. When he was within striking distance, he leapt, tackling the human from behind. The human hardly budged – Vox didn't have enough mass to knock the human over, but that was not what he had been trying to do. The human whipped around, more startled than anything. As he did, he brought his arms out in front of him, an instinctive defensive reaction. With them came the car keys, jangling at the end the human's fingers. Vox quickly jumped and grabbed them with his jaws, and then took off, down the road. The human blundered around for a moment, confused. Then, the human noticed Vox, and yelled at him. Vox heard, but didn't look back. He just kept running down the road. He would have to be fast if this was to work.

Vox kept an ear out for approaching traffic. He couldn't hear any, and so he darted across the T-junction, to the gutter on the other side. He glanced back up the road. The human was running towards him, but carefully, as it was down a slope, and running down a slope with only two legs did not offer much stability.

Vox purposefully dropped the keys in the gutter, making sure the human could see him do so. Another loud and angry yell escaped from the human. Vox immediately began running back across the T-junction and up the road. The human slowed down, seeing Vox coming at him. Good, this would buy Vox some time. Without reducing his speed, Vox rushed past the human, continuing to run uphill. The human turned to look at Vox, perplexed, but then turned and continued down the road, towards the gutter, where the car keys had been dropped. Vox, in the meantime, ran towards the car.

As soon as Vox reached the car, he turned and jumped into the open door. He clambered onto the seat with the steering wheel, and looked in between the front seats. There was the gear stick and the handbrake. Quickly, Vox grabbed the handbrake in between his jaws and pulled upwards. Then, using one of his front paws, he pushed down on the button at the end of the handbrake. Maintaining his pressure on the button, he moved his head down, allowing the handbrake to lower.

The car immediately lurched forwards. Vox let go of the handbrake and jumped out of the car, just as the door swung shut. The car was rolling down the road, much faster than Vox had anticipated; but that was ok.

The human had reached the gutter, and was squatting over it. He appeared to be reluctant to fish around for his keys, but he quickly found them. He picked them up and tried to wipe off some of the mud and slime. That's when he seemed to notice the noise of the car rolling down the hill. He turned his head, only to see his car barrelling towards him. He let out an exclamation, but was cut off. There was a thump, then a crunch, and then a red star exploded out from between the car and the wall. A delicate fragrance of blood and bile drifted through the air.

Vox turned and ran back the way he had come.

Vox soon returned to the restaurant where the other two formerly-masked humans were eating. They were still digging into their food, unaware of the demise of their cohort. Thankfully, the human ability to know things about their greater vicinity didn't seem to have taken effect yet. However, that had also probably been because of the lack of other humans at the time. In any case, there was no time to waste; and Vox had a plan.

Vox went and stood in plain view of the two humans. They looked up from their food, and at him. He felt a shiver or apprehension run down his spine. The humans looked at each other, and then exchanged some words. One of the humans stood up – from his smell, it wasn't the gun-wielding human, but one of the other ones. Vox noticed that this one had a bandage wrapped around his hand. This was the one that Vox had bitten.

Vox turned around and began trotting away, looking backwards at the humans. The bandaged human was following him. He smelled angry. Vox picked up his pace slightly. He glanced backwards. The human was running towards him. Startled, Vox fled.

Vox rushed in the direction of the bridge. He could hear the bandaged human's footsteps behind him. He was getting tired, having already run down and up the road. An angry shout followed him. He ran faster.

Soon, Vox had reached the bridge. The heavy footsteps of the bandaged human were still steady behind him. Vox darted towards the safety fence that ran down the side of the bridge. He squeezed through the bars. He turned around to look at the human chasing him. The human stopped in front of the bars, glaring at Vox. Then, the human leapt onto the fence and began clambering over.

Vox turned and darted towards the edge of the bridge. He slowed down as he came to the edge of the rough concrete. He looked down. A metal girder ran down the side of the bridge. Vox looked back. The human had just landed on this side of the safety fence. Vox turned towards the edge of the bridge, and then stepped off, onto the smooth metal girder. It was not very wide, so he had to be extremely careful. Keeping his weight evenly distributed, he walked down the girder, towards the head of one of the support pylons. He didn't dare look back, lest he lose balance. However, he could hear the human still pursuing him, intermittently muttering and yelling at him. The human's pace had slowed significantly, though, as the human would find it even more difficult to walk down the thin girder.

The girder expanded into a small platform in front of Vox, right above the pylon. Vox carefully made his way there. Just before he stepped onto the platform, he stopped and released his bladder. It was easy, aided by the rather precarious position he was in. Then, he stepped forwards, onto the relatively safe platform.

Vox turned around. The human was coming towards him faster than Vox had expected. He was certainly motivated.

As the human neared Vox, he saw the urine on the girder. He stepped over it, probably since humans tend to dislike stepping onto defecation. His front leg was almost on the platform that Vox was on.

Vox stretched out and snapped at the human's foot. He didn't even need to touch the human: having already been bitten, the human reacted by jerking backwards, shifting his weight onto his back foot, which slipped slightly on the metal girder. The human immediately compensated for the slight slip by re-shifting his weight onto his front foot, which he placed right on top of the puddle of urine. The sudden shifts in weight had caused him to sway slightly. Ordinarily, this swaying would have been corrected by the weight-shifting itself. However, due to the lubricated surface, his front foot slipped.

The human slipped, smacking the side of his head into the metal girder, and then fell right off the girder. His scream petered away as he fell, until there was a splattering sound of flesh against rock.

Vox carefully made his way back onto the bridge. From there, he squeezed through the safety fence, and headed back towards the restaurant, where the last of the formerly-masked humans was. The gun-wielding human.

The gun-wielding human saw Vox coming towards the patio. He seemed baffled that Vox had returned and the bandaged human hadn't. He reached into his pocket and pulled out a phone. He stared at the phone, twiddling at it with his thumbs. Was he trying to find out what happened to his cohort? Vox didn't want to wait to find out.

He dashed forwards, towards the gun-wielding human, but as silently as he could. The human was engrossed with his phone. Vox ran up onto the patio, towards the table. The human noticed him and looked up from his phone. Vox darted under the table. The human quickly pushed back his chair and stood up, looking down at the ground below the table. Vox came out from under the table, right in front of the human. The human kicked at Vox, but it was a flimsy kick and Vox easily managed to sidestep it. Instead, Vox lunged at the human's ankles, growling and snapping. The human jumped back, kicking his chair over. He snapped his head back, watching his steps so that he didn't trip over the chair. Vox seized this opportunity, leaping up and grabbing the phone out of the human's hand. He felt its lukewarm tasteless plastic between his teeth. Clenching down, he turned and scampered off.

Vox rushed out of the cluster of restaurants. He could hear the human running after him. He made sure to stay on the roads, so that the human could follow him. He headed towards the woods that ran along the river. As his surroundings transitioned from urban to arboreal, he left the roads, but made sure that he took the widest, most easily traversable paths. He didn't want to discourage the human from pursuing him.

The sound of the human's footsteps was growing more distant. Vox stopped, and turned back towards the human. The human was slowing down. The reduction in disincentive might have been working, but the human needed more incentive. Vox dropped the phone on the ground, for the human to see. Then, Vox reached down and began chewing on it. He felt the plastic crack under the force of his mastication. With an angry yell, the human picked up his pace and again began running after Vox. Vox immediately picked the phone up again, turned around, and ran deeper into the woods.

Soon, Vox smelt it: the metal beast. It lay ahead, and Vox remembered where. He ran towards it location, treading carefully and keeping his nose alert. As he approached the close-set group of trees, he slowed down to a trot. The human was still running, quickly gaining ground on him. Vox cautiously navigated around the close-set trees. The smell of the rusted metal was strong from the centre, which was now exactly between Vox and the human coming after him.

The human's face poked through the middle of the close-set trees. He was panting, winded, but furious. The stink of his sweat and adrenaline was palpable, and his face was twisted into a grimace. Seeing Vox standing there, the human pointed at him and yelled. Vox didn't move. The human pushed through the shrubbery, stepping in between the trees.

With a snap, the metal beast sprang into action. Its jaws clenched around the human's leg, and a crack echoed out, through the woods. The human screamed in agony.

Still holding the phone between his teeth, Vox fled, leaving the human and his screams far behind.

Jay washed his hands, having just finished cleaning the house and yard. As he was drying them on the kitchen towel, his phone vibrated. Jay reached into his pocket and pulled it out. The call was from the local police station. Jay quickly answered.

"Hello?"

"It's me again." replied the deputy. She had been corresponding with Jay for the last two weeks, since the break-in. "I have some news"

Jay pulled up one of the chairs in the kitchen and sat down. "I'm listening"

"We got them. All of them"

A wave of relief swept over Jay, but he tried not to make it too apparent. "That's really good" he said evenly.

"Yes, their prints match the ones in your house, as well as a number of other homi… er… home invasions."

The deputy had stumbled over that word. Homicides? There had been a number of other… Jay grimaced.

The deputy continued: "We even found the weapon. Ballistics matches the bullets we collected from your house."

Jay nodded. "Sounds like you've got an open and shut case."

"Pretty much." mused the deputy. "The only thing we have out of place is a cell phone that belongs to one of the suspects."

"I take it that these… that they're going to go away for life?"

"Not really." said the deputy.

Jay's brow furrowed. "What do you mean? How… how can they be let go? They tried to kill my daughter…"

The deputy interrupted him. "That's not what I meant." she said. "Sorry, what I meant is that they won't need to go to prison. The suspects were found… deceased."

Jay's eyes widened. "Wow…" he said and stopped. He was not sure what to say.

"Yep. Darwin awards, all over." said the deputy.

"What do you mean?" asked Jay.

"They seemed to have… killed themselves in really stupid ways." explained the deputy. "One fell off the local bridge. No idea what he was trying to do. Another got run over by his own car. Forgot to set his parking brake all the way. And the last one was just found, caught in a hunting trap. Died of dehydration. That one was slightly weird. He didn't have his phone on him; if he had, he might have been able to call for help. Oddly enough, he had just sent a text to his friend who fell of the bridge. But now, the phone is nowhere to be found." The deputy paused. Then: "I'm not supposed to be telling you this." she quickly added. "But, I figured that you should know that you're not on the hook."

Jay nodded again. He hadn't even considered that their deaths might have caused problems for him. "Thank you for telling me."

"No problem. I can only imagine how this must have been for you and your family." replied the deputy.

"Tara… she's my life. And that night… if it hadn't been for Vox…" Jay trailed off.

"Vox? That's your dog, right?" asked the deputy.

"Yeah, that's him." said Jay. Jay got up and headed to the doorway. He looked out. Vox lay sprawled out in the middle of the yard, soaking in the sun.

"Does he bark a lot?" asked the deputy.

"No… not at all." said Jay, slightly thrown by the question. "Why do you ask?"

"Doesn't Vox mean 'voice' in Latin?"

Jay laughed. "Ah, yes. You're right. It does. But actually, that's just his nickname." he explained.

"So what's his real name?" she asked.

"Actually, his name is Havoc. When we first got him, Tara was too young to pronounce it correctly. She called him Vox, and that name stuck." A glint from the corner of the yard caught Jay's eye. Instinctively, he worried that it was a piece of glass, or something that might hurt Tara. He walked out into the yard, and headed towards the corner.

"Why Havoc?" asked the deputy. "Was he much trouble?"

"Quite the opposite." said Jay. "I keep telling people the story of how he got toilet trained in two days flat, and nobody believes me."

"That… is quite impressive."

"Yeah, he's really great." Jay bent down and ran his fingers over Vox's head. "To answer your question, though. My wife, while she was still with us, she always wanted to get a dog. Now, being an English teacher, she was quite fond of Shakespeare. She loved the play Julius Caesar. Are you familiar with it?" Jay had reached the corner of the yard. He knelt down to examine the source of the glint. A small shiny piece of plastic poked out of the ground, having been half buried.

"Not really." admitted the deputy. "Literature was never my strong suit."

"Well, there is this passage in the play." Jay continued explaining. At the same time, he picked up a nearby stick and poked at the plastic in the earth. It was part of a larger plastic shape. A phone, half buried in the ground. "Julius Caesar has just been killed by assassins, and his right-hand man, Antony, gives this long speech about it. You might have heard about it. 'Friends, Romans, Countrymen, lend me your ears…'?"

"I think I know what you're talking about." said the deputy.

"My wife loved this particular speech. Specifically, these lines…" Jay reached down and pulled the phone out of the ground. The battery was dead, and the chassis had been chewed on. He held the phone up, looking at it. At first, he wondered where it had come from. Then, he turned back to look at Vox lying in the sun, comprehension dawning over him, even as he continued explaining to the deputy. "...'And Caesar's spirit, raging for revenge,\ With Ate by his side come hot from hell,\ Shall in these confines with a monarch's voice\ Cry "Havoc!" and let slip the dogs of war'...".

***